TO THE CITY, WITH LOVE

Volume II

by

Steve Slavin

TO THE CITY, WITH LOVE
Volume II

Published by
Fat Dog Books
California, USA

Fat Dog Books
ISBN: 978-0-9991370-2-4

Literature & Fiction/Contemporary/Short Story Collection
Printed in the United States of America

Visit our website at www.fatdogbooks.com

ACKNOWLEDGMENTS

First and foremost, I want to thank my publisher and editor, Michael Stringer, for all his help and encouragement. As virtually every fiction writer will tell you, it is extremely difficult to get a short story collection published. Not only did Michael give me that chance, but he was able to convert a pile of stories into a book.

My high school friend, Linda Sperling, not only edited most of these stories, but she supplied scores of extremely helpful suggestions. A great storyteller, she has supplied me with numerous ideas which I shamelessly borrowed.

Chuck Stickney, another of my high school friends, made dozens of very helpful suggestions, and makes a few personal appearances in this collection.

Jacqueline Seewald, another writer, generously shared her extensive experience publicizing and selling her work.

I also want to thank all my friends who provided story ideas. Among them were Barbara Hanna, Len Friedman, Kathy Rehm, Krista Van Laan, Nancy Zanca, Dianna Goldberg, Peggy Deane, Marshall Anker, Arnie Schwartz, Patti Amour, Nora Edwards, Donna Sommer, John Berbrich, Mary Rae Thewlis, Deana Dauber, Arnie Schwartz, Paul Diamond, and Don Gobere.

Finally, I want to thank my sister, Leontine Temsky, for taking the cover photo, and my nieces, Eleni Zimiles, Liz Zimiles, Justine Zimiles, and Sophie Zimiles, for their very helpful comments about my stories.

The heart and soul of short story publishing are the small literary magazines, which consider submissions from unknown writers. Almost every story in this book appeared in one of the magazines listed here. I want to thank each of their editors, not just for publishing my work, but for their helpful criticism and encouragement.

Amateur Writers Journal, A New Ulster Magazine, Arts Tree House, Barbaric Yawp, Bareback Magazine, Bitchin' Kitsch, Calliope, Donut Factory Express, Horror Sleaze Trash, Indiana Voice Journal, Mad Swirl, Mgversiondeux Datura, Origami, Paragon Journal, Penny Shorts, PKA's Advocate, Section 8, Sign of the Times, Temptation Magazine, The Blotter Magazine, The Literary Yard, The Short Humour Site, The Small Pond, The Starving Artist, Work Literary Magazine, Work Magazine, Writers Block, Writing Raw, and *Ygdrasi.*

TABLE OF CONTENTS

INTRODUCTION

If Paris is the city of love, then what is New York? Perhaps New York is the city of unimaginable possibilities. *I* should know. Almost every weekend my friends and I would go to parties, never knowing where we'd end up, or who we would end up *with*.

The only thing we knew for sure was that we would have a lot of fun. Perhaps that explains how some PR flak came up with a nick-name for New York—Fun City. It may be stupid-sounding, and yet it was an apt description.

Most of my stories took place in the 1960s, 1970s, and 1980s. Ancient history? Sure, it is! Yuh gotta problem with that?

The city is very different today—much more expensive, younger, and certainly more cynical. But then again, every generation looks back and concludes that *they* had had the best of times.

So, I hope that you have as much fun reading about all things that *we* did as we had doing them.

Part I

PARTY ANIMALS

From the mid-1960s through the mid-1980s, almost every weekend my friends and I went to several parties a night, never knowing who we would meet or where we would end up. It seemed as though the City was just one big party. It's ironic that "party" became a verb in the 1980s, because that's when the party scene began to wind down. Those certainly *were* the days, my friend.

UNCLE BEN

"Hello, Sophia? This is your Uncle Ben. Could I buy you a cup of coffee and a sandwich? "

That's my roommate, Ben, asking out a 'girl.' That girl was probably in her fifties, and Ben himself had to be pushing sixty. Would you believe he actually fought in World War II? Which was what, over 20 years ago?

OK, you're thinking what would a young guy like me, just out of college, be doing with a roommate like Ben? Do I have to draw you a road map? It's simple. I have no money. Actually, I have a job, but I just started last week, so I haven't seen my first paycheck. Of course, when you're an assistant editor at a medium-sized magazine, perhaps 'paycheck' is not the best way to describe your compensation. What they are paying me is more like an allowance.

Did you ever wonder how young editors can make it in New York? Well, they don't, unless they happen to have trust funds. And the rest of us live with roommates. But when you're really at the bottom of the barrel, you live with Uncle Ben.

Ben told me that he had run an ad in the *Village Voice*, and guys would come over to his place, take one look at him and say, "Forget it!" No one wanted a roommate almost three times his age. Well, *almost* no one.

So how did I meet Ben? Funny you should ask. My friend, Paul, who I knew from high school? He used to invite me to his family gatherings for years, and it was there I'd run into Uncle Ben. Even back then, he had those unruly tufts of white hair sticking straight out from the sides of his head. On top, he was completely bald. And for some reason, he always wore a powder blue pullover sweater. I don't know if he bought a bunch of them on sale or if he kept wearing the same one.

Ben was the life of these family gatherings, and all of Paul's relatives loved him. He seemed to have an unending repertoire of stories, jokes, and wisecracks.

"Hey, did you heat *this* one?" and, as soon as his audience stopped laughing he had another one, and then another.

One day. I asked Paul if Ben was his mother's brother or his father's brother. Well, it turns out that Uncle Ben wasn't even related. A long time ago—no one seems to remember exactly when—Ben just started coming to these gatherings, and pretty soon they were calling him Uncle Ben. Now here's the kicker: Ben isn't even his name.

"So why does everyone call him Ben?" I asked. "Because of the way his hair sticks up. He looks like Ben-Gurion."

In case you're not up on Israeli history, David Ben-Gurion was one of the Founding Fathers of Israel, and a long-serving prime minister. And it was true Uncle Ben was a dead ringer for Ben-Gurion. They must have gone to the same hair stylist. Instead of asking how much do you want me to take off, the stylist must have asked, how high do you want it to stick up?

I kind of wondered why Ben would want a roommate, since the rent was only $80 a month. It didn't take me long to figure it out. Ben hated to work. Sometimes, I'd get home from work, and he was still in bed. He wasn't depressed or anything, but he often slept all day, claiming that the alarm never went off.

One day he announced, "We're having a party! Invite everyone!"

And so we did. By 9 o'clock, the place was mobbed. There were people of all ages, people who looked like they just walked in off the street, guys in suits, hippies, freaks—everyone. And in walks this woman who announces that she is Mrs. Sam Schlockman.

"Yeah," I say to her, "and your point is...?"

"I am *Mrs.* Sam Schlockman."

Then Ben walks over to her, puts his arms around her, and kisses her on the cheek. It turns out she's his *wife.* And *he's* Sam Schlockman.

Hey, given my druthers, I guess *I'd* rather be Uncle Ben.

All of a sudden, she's crying. "Sam, how could you leave me? After all the years I've supported you."

Then, one of the women gently guides her into the other room to calm her down, which was just as well, because there was Ben, chatting up another woman. But not for long. This really dried up old woman named Maria—she looked like a pale prune—starts berating Ben.

"How could you *do* this to me? You never told me you were married. I thought your name was Ben."

I have to give *this* to the guy. He handled it. He took her out in the hall to talk, and when they came in a few minutes later, they were all lovey-dovey.

The party ended pretty late, and Ben took his wife home and didn't return till the next afternoon. He explained that he had never really gotten even a legal separation, but that they had "an understanding." And what about that other woman?

"Maria? Oh, she's cool with it."

He and Maria had been an item on and off for years, but somehow, Ben had never gotten around to mentioning anything about *Mrs.* Sam Schlockman.

The next evening when I came home from work, I noticed the kitchen table and chairs were missing. And so was the TV. Were we *robbed?* Not likely, since nothing else seemed to be taken. Then I heard the key in the lock. It was Ben with still another 'girl.'

She was at least 70 if she was a day. But hey, Ben was no spring chicken either, so I guess it was no big deal. Maybe it was that polka dot dress that got to me. Or the orthopedic shoes. But it definitely was not the time to say anything about the missing furniture. So I told him I was going out and wouldn't be back till late. We had this agreement about giving each other privacy.

Finally, Ben and I caught up with each other the next day. "So, what's the story with the kitchen table and chairs and the TV?"

Ben told me that Maria had a key and must have taken them. It turns out she had bought this stuff for Ben as a kind of housewarming present. I guess she wasn't that cool about Ben's wife after all.

A day or two later, Ben informed me that he was moving back in with his wife, and that I could have the apartment. What he didn't bother mentioning was that he had been fired weeks ago and had run out of money.

Every so often the phone would ring, and it would be one of the 'girls' looking for Ben. I told them I'd give him the message, but I never did. Still, I kind of miss the guy. I mean, where could I ever find another roommate like Uncle Ben?

A MEDICAL QUESTION

The party was so crowded that not a single additional person could fit into the room. If I had held my drink straight out, eight or ten people could have had a sip.

Everyone could easily hear each of the conversations around them. In fact, when the woman with whom I was talking mentioned that she was a nurse, a guy across the room began waving his arms and then pointing at her.

She shrugged and then pointed at herself. He nodded vigorously and then began the arduous journey across the room. Then he stopped, and cupping his hands around his mouth, he called out, "You're a nurse, right?"

She nodded.

Inching his way through the crowd, he seemed to grow increasingly agitated. He stopped again and called out, "You're *sure* you're a nurse?"

She smiled, emphatically shaking her head "yes."

"Do you think he's having some kind of medical emergency?" I asked.

"I seriously doubt it. But then again, you never know."

As I watched him, I visualized a crowd passing his body through a mosh pit. But this poor soul was clearly overdressed in his three-piece suit.

Finally, he managed to squeeze past the last few people, and found himself standing face-to-face with us.

"So, you're absolutely *sure* you're a nurse?"

"Would you like to see some ID?"

"No, no! Of course not!"

"May I ask *you* a question?"

"Shoot!" he replied.

"I'm very flattered that you went to all the trouble of squeezing through this crowd. But I'm completely puzzled as to why you kept asking if I was a nurse."

He didn't say anything. But he appeared to think that his question was completely logical. How could she *not* understand why this was so important to him?

She and I waited expectantly. Finally, he wet his lips, swallowed, took a deep breath, and proceeded to clear up the great mystery.

"My name's Melvin. I'm a doctor."

KING OF THE PARTY CIRCUIT

Marvin Loopawitz had it all. A bachelor pad in Brooklyn Heights, just a couple of blocks off the promenade. A cushy professorship at New York University, which required his teaching just one course a semester. But best of all, Marvin had all the beautiful women he could possibly want— and then some.

He drove a vintage Oldsmobile 88, was extraordinarily devoted to his mother, and in his spare time, he found loving homes for little kittens. But first and foremost, Marvin was the "King of the Party Circuit."

You're probably thinking that Marvin was just too good to be true. And you'd be right. He *was*. So, I'm going to level with you. After all, you know that appearances can sometimes be deceiving.

Marvin *did* live in a nice apartment in Brooklyn Heights, and he was indeed quite devoted to his dear old mother. In fact, he actually *lived* with her. Now somewhere in his fifties or sixties, he still "lived at home." Not that there's anything *wrong* with that.

His bachelor pad was a comfortable three-room apartment in a residential hotel. His mother had the bedroom, and Marvin slept on a high riser in the kitchen. The entire apartment was filled with his mother's huge collection of knick-knacks that covered every flat surface.

Every Monday, his mother would give him a list of things to buy in the supermarket, and then she would supervise his meal preparations for the rest of the week. Marvin was a good boy who followed instructions. Mrs. Loopawitz did not know what she would have done without him. And vice versa.

At 9 o'clock every Friday morning he would drive his mother to his sister's house in Queens. She'd spend the weekend there, and then on Monday morning, he'd drive her back home again.

I met Mrs. Loopawitz one morning when Marvin was opening the car door for her. She seemed a pleasant woman, perhaps in her late eighties. The term, "old biddy," came to mind—as did an even less charitable description—a few years past her expiration date. In fact, some of Marvin's friends—and I'll admit to having been among them—sometimes speculated about who would die first, Marvin or his mother.

The vintage Oldsmobile he drove was a cast-off from his brother-in-law. Its exterior was rusted, and there were large holes in the floor. But he was still able to drive it, and liked to tell people that he had had a lot of great offers for it, but he refused to sell.

The teaching position at NYU was the only job Marvin ever had. He was not exactly a professor. Back in the 1950s, he occasionally taught a speech course for the division of adult education, but he was let go after just a few semesters. But luckily, he didn't really *have* to support himself since he "lived at home." He not only had free room and board, but his parents provided him with a very nice allowance. There *had* been a short rough patch when his father died, but he left more than enough money for his wife and son to get by without him.

I once asked Marvin if he had been in World War II. A couple of times he had mentioned being "just a kid" during the War, but in a moment of candor, Marvin confessed that he had done something to his foot to avoid getting drafted. Maybe that's why he walked with a slight limp.

The part of Marvin's life about finding homes for kittens *was* completely true. Years before, he had gotten a Canadian woman pregnant, and she had an abortion. He had begged her to have the child—not that he would have been willing or able to provide for its support—let alone offer his hand in matrimony. Maybe it was a form of atonement to devote himself to "rescuing homeless little kitties."

Brooklyn Heights had several residential hotels, and occasionally pregnant cats would find their way into their basements. The hotel managers were happy to let Marvin and a few other animal lovers take the kittens off their hands. On Saturday afternoons, they had a table on Montague Street—the main thoroughfare of the Heights. On the table was a box of kittens and a sign, "Free kittens seeking loving homes."

Now that you know all about Marvin, let's talk about the Party Circuit. Each year during the 1960s, tens of thousands of young people moved to New York, and the city became a great party town. And through the Party Circuit, Marvin, I, and a bunch of other guys—and a handful of women—were plugged into the party scene.

Here's how the circuit worked. If you knew about a party, you gave the information to Marvin—the address, the starting time, whether you needed to bring a bottle, and, most important, a name you could use that would help get you in. You'd arrive at the party, and tell the host or hostess you were invited by so-and-so. If Marvin didn't have a name you could use, he would give you that party on a "crash basis." In other words, you could try to sweet talk your way in.

It didn't really matter if you got turned away. You'd just go to the next party on your list. Even if you *did* get in, you probably didn't want to stay too long because there were several other parties you wanted to hit. In fact, the people on the circuit called themselves runners because they were always running from party to party. Some of them spent more time *between* parties than at the parties themselves. What drove them was never knowing what they might be missing.

Think of the party circuit as a cooperative organization, with Marvin operating the switchboard. Late one Saturday afternoon, for example, a friend of a friend had a gallery opening, and my friend and I were invited to a party to be held in the artist's loft that evening. I called Marvin with the information. When we arrived a couple of hours later, the place was packed. About half the guests were from the circuit. Marvin was at the door. A drink in one hand and a cigarette in the other, he graciously welcomed us: "Glad you could make it."

Marvin sometimes joked that running the circuit was a full-time job. He was on the phone every evening of the week, hearing about parties and spreading the word. By Friday night, his biggest problem was trying to get to all the parties on his list.

Marvin was of an indeterminate age. He could have been a really old-looking 45, or maybe he just looked his age, which might have been 65. As soon as he arrived at a party, he'd head right over to the nearest attractive young woman, whip out his pen and pad, and say, "Let me put you between two clean white sheets." An older woman once overheard him and said to the younger woman, "Do you realize how *old* this man is?" Marvin gave her a scornful look and said, "When I'm as old as *you* are, I'll be dead."

To say that Marvin drank like a fish and smoked like a chimney would just begin to describe how much he abused his body. He never exercised, stayed up till 3 or 4 am, never ate any fruit or vegetables, and, to top things off, he never walked when he could drive. By the time the city of New York made it a lot harder to be a smoker or drinker, Marvin had, perhaps mercifully, passed on. But from the mid-1960s through the mid-1980s, he was the king.

You may be wondering how well Marvin did with the women. Let's *face* it: How was an older, out-of-shape alcoholic who lived with his mother and never really had a job supposed to get dates, let alone even occasionally find a woman who would go to bed with him? Do you recall the youth mantra of those times: Never trust anyone over thirty? Well Marvin followed his *own* version of that: Never *date* anyone over thirty.

At a Sunday afternoon party out in Queens, we met a beautiful woman in her early twenties. Her name was Doffy, and she had the bluest eyes I had ever seen. She truly could have been a movie star. Marvin was utterly smitten and had managed to get her phone number.

On the way home, I asked Marvin if he was in love with her.

"Are you *kidding*? How could I *not* be?"

"So, if she wanted to move in with you, would you let her?" OK, I *was* being a little cruel, maybe thinking if there would be enough room for her on his high riser in the kitchen.

But Marvin didn't catch on. He was too much in love. "Of course! If she really wanted to live with me, then nothing could make me happier."

"OK, so if she actually moved in with you, how long would you let her stay?"

Quick as a flash, he answered, "Oh, maybe about a month."

So how did a man with so little going for him even hope to get *any* woman, let alone a woman as lovely as Doffy? And does he run to all these parties actually expecting to meet—if not the woman of his dreams—then maybe the woman of the month?

Everyone needs love, even dirty old men. But not everyone *gets* love. So the million dollar question with respect to Marvin was: How did he *do* it?

He did it by playing the numbers. Every weekend he went to about ten parties—five on Friday night and five on Saturday night. He would get the numbers of a few young women at each party. *How?*

"Hello, I'm Marvin. Do you like parties?" Of course she did. "I hear about a lot of parties." Which was certainly true. "Give me your number and when I hear of some, I'll call you." An offer she could not refuse. What young woman would want to turn down her party godfather?

On Sunday evenings, he'd start making his calls. He'd invite each woman to his apartment for dinner on the following weekend—mentioning that he was a "dynamite cook" —and then he would take her to a bunch of parties. Usually, of course, the woman saw through his ploy, and ask why she couldn't just meet him at one of the parties. No problem: He'd just call the next one on the list. That's why he needed to take all those numbers.

How many women fell for the dinner line and came to his apartment? Maybe 1 in 20. He was very efficient about making these dinners. It was always chili—his best and only dish. He'd cook up several pounds, divide it up into individual meals which he put into freezer, and he was all set for several dates.

When the woman arrived at his apartment—remember, Mrs. Loopawitz was at her daughter's house for the weekend—Marvin had turned the place into his version of a bachelor pad. To set the mood, he had put 25-watt red bulbs in all the lamps, and then threw most of his mother's knick knacks into her bedroom. Marvin had a ready answer when a woman would remark that the place looked like an old lady's apartment: My mother sometimes stays with me.

After dinner Marvin would make his move. Most women handled this very well, by simply saying that they already had a boyfriend, or that it was much too soon, and couldn't they get to know each other a little better before they did anything? That was just fine with Marvin, because he *did* have all those parties to go to.

So, they'd go downstairs and get into his car, which he kept parked right outside the door. They'd go to the first party on the list, and within half an hour Marvin was on his way to the next one. Sometime later, his "date" might be wondering what had happened to him.

Did Marvin ever score? Well, there's an old saying in baseball, that if you go to bat enough times, eventually you might actually hit the ball. And every so often, he *did* get lucky. He told me that for every five hundred phone numbers that he took, maybe *one* woman actually went to bed with him. He didn't say how may chili dinners he had provided. But if he were playing baseball, his batting average would be .002, which comes to a success rate of just two tenths of one percent.

As the saying goes, "All good things must come to an end," and so it was with the party circuit. By the mid-1980s we were hearing about fewer and fewer parties. Whether it was the growing fear of AIDS, or that people were making fewer parties, or maybe that we were all getting older, the circuit grew smaller and smaller, and much less active. Even Marvin dropped away and we lost touch.

Then, one day I got a call from one of the long-time runners. Marvin had died. *When?* About a year ago.

Well, I thought, he had lived a good life. How many of us can create our own fantasy world and actually get to live in it? To grow old without ever having to grow up?

Back in the days when Marvin was still king, some of us used to wonder: Who would go first, Marvin or his mother? I suppose that now we'll never know.

THE BROKEN MAN

There's a man I've seen at countless parties. A man who, you might say, has long suffered from broken health. He's in his early fifties, but very stooped, and forced to use a cane. No one knows exactly what's wrong with him, only that he's in and out of hospitals.

The man is an idealist, or perhaps it would be more precise to call him a purist. He is searching for the perfect woman—for *him*, that is. Of course, she must be beautiful, charming and *very* bright. But more important, she must be a witty conversationalist, a vibrant, outgoing and sympathetic person. Only such a woman could please him.

I've wondered why he went on his way, so lonely and forlorn. Why he had set up such exacting and unreasonable requirements. Why he didn't settle for someone less wonderful? Or if he was really afraid of involvement. And then, too, just who did he think he was, expecting, or even hoping, that such an ideal woman would even look at him? He was homely, he was ill, and *most* unforgivably, he was dull. No one could stand having a conversation with this man for more than a few minutes. He would hardly say anything, and you would be left doing all the talking, trying desperately to fill every long awkward silence and dead space. So we wondered what anyone could find attractive in this poor old man.

He had been born somewhere in Central Europe and was evidently a refugee. Now in some sort of business for himself, he was moderately well-to-do. He usually wore conservatively tailored dark blue suits, which provided a neutral background for our multi-colored body shirts.

He would occasionally engage a woman in conversation, listen for a while, and then wander off into some corner where he would spend the rest of the evening. Once or twice he took a phone number, but never left with a woman. Most of the time he'd be off in some corner, sitting quietly, watching the party.

The rest of us had somewhat less exacting requirements. If a woman were reasonably attractive and if her vocation were more exotic than, say, elementary school teacher, there'd be two or three of us after her phone number. Except for a few parties out in Brooklyn and several on the Upper East Side, we would certainly encounter our fair share of half-way decent women. But on very rare occasions, perhaps once every few months, a truly outstanding woman—a woman who would actually be acceptable to the poor broken man—would unexpectedly turn up at some party. Of course, several of us would crowd around her, or else make our moves in teams of two or three. Some women exulted in this attention, others regally accepted it as their due, while still others smilingly parried our ardent verbal thrusts.

Not long ago I arrived rather late to one of these parties and was quickly on the make. There she was, sitting in the corner with a couple of guys who were coming on to her. I waited until one of them stood up, having come away empty-handed after several attempts upon her phone number. As I took his seat, I smiled and told her that the coach had sent in the first team. She seemed amused and encouraged me to go on. While I was filling her in on some of the more interesting aspects of my autobiography, the other guy got up and his place was soon taken by the broken man.

Now I was in. The chase was over. In fact, I'd be a sport and wouldn't even take her number. What for, since I'd be leaving with her?

Everything went according to plan—at least for a few minutes. I had been telling her about some research I'd been

26

doing when she asked me if I'd go get her another drink. When I got back she and the broken man were talking. Fine, I thought: at least one of my so-called friends hadn't moved in on me. I listened for a while, but their conversation was pretty boring. They didn't exclude me or anything, but I just didn't feel like listening. Still, I forced myself to stay put. I figured she was just trying to be nice to him.

They kept talking and I started to drift off. I thought of how this man had gone to hundreds of parties, but never met anyone. And now he finally did. Of all the women, why did he have to pick *this* one? This guy had absolutely no chance to get her number, but meanwhile he was killing *my* chances,

Oh well, she really wasn't all the great. I mean, I doubt if we'd have actually hit it off. I want a woman to appreciate me, but if she goes for a guy like that… but for what it was worth, I just sat there and waited. I wanted her to tell me later, "Steve, did you think I could possibly be attracted to that poor guy? I mean, he's nice, but I could never possibly see myself with him."

It was getting late and there weren't any other decent women left. Maybe she wasn't all that bad even if she *did* go on and on. I never heard a female talk as much as this one did, but I had to admit, she had a head on her shoulders, if you know what I mean. Boy, once she was finished with that guy, I just wanted to take her out of this place. *Then* we'd really get to know each other—if you catch my drift.

Sometimes you see just what you want to see. Sometimes you make up things that just aren't there. The three of us had been sitting there for maybe an hour, but I must have been somewhere else most of the time. And now it was too late. Finally they got up to go. I stood too, and for a moment she and I were alone. I just said, "Why?"

She smiled and shook her head.

"Are you happy?"

She nodded.

"Why?"

"You probably wouldn't understand."

27

"Try me," I said.

"He listens."

MY NIGHT AT MENSA

1

One day, completely out of the blue, my neighbor Karen invited me to a Mensa party. We were friendly, but we never really socialized. She did something in computers, was recently divorced, and is a little older than me.

I knew that Mensa was a high-IQ organization, and that some of its members were kind of eccentric. Still, Karen was nice, so if *she* thought I would have a good time, why not give it a shot? When she mentioned that there would be some attractive women at the party that definitely clinched the deal.

The night before the party I decided to do a quick Internet search. I learned that Mensa's only entrance requirement was scoring in the top two percent on most standard IQ tests. And that Mensans loved jokes—even those at their own expense.

I found an anecdote about a talk delivered by the head of a local Phi Beta Kappa chapter to a large group of Mensans. She began by announcing, "I am so happy to be here representing an organization of *over*achievers… to address an organization of …." After a pause of just two or three seconds, people started laughing. Soon the entire audience was in hysterics. They *got* the joke! After all, they were *Mensans*! I later learned that Mensans liked to say that one of the great things about their organization was not having to explain their jokes. Maybe they should have joined a comedian's club like the Friars.

Since passing an IQ test was the sole entrance requirement, Mensans are an amazingly eclectic group. There are the highly educated and the high school dropouts, movie stars and complete nerds, the rich and the poor, and people holding every possible religious, social, and political viewpoint. And, of course, there are the members who no other group would accept.

2

On the cab ride downtown, Karen filled me in on some of the Mensa characters. "We definitely have our share of losers and social misfits."

"I guess I can deal with that."

"Jerry, we'll see if you feel that way after meeting Big Mike. And looks *can* be deceiving. Mike is tall, quite good looking, and actually seems normal. That is, until you see him eat."

"How bad can he be? Does he smack his lips and spray his food?"

"Well once, when we had a bowl of onion soup dip that was almost empty, Big Mike licked out the bowl."

"Gross!"

"Jerry, don't let me get started! So there's this other guy. He's known as 'Orange Man.'"

"Does he juggle oranges and catch them in his mouth?"

"Good try! For starters, he dresses completely in orange— shirt, tie, pants, belt, socks, and even his shoes. And when he eats M & Ms, he picks his way through the entire bowl, selecting just the orange ones."

"Big Mike and Orange Man sound like loads of fun."

"You want *fun*? Try the Flashlight Lady. She's got to be at least 80, looks like a witch, and shines this flashlight on everything she eats to purify it."

"Maybe she just needs to *see* her food."

"No, Jerry. She once gave this lecture about it. She told everyone that some foods were pure, some were poisonous, and some were toxic but could be purified.

"Karen, you're telling me that Mensa let her lecture?"

"This was at our local convention. We had lots of speakers, and there was probably almost no vetting. Besides, the title of her talk was not nearly as far out as the keynoter's address, "How to raise your IQ by holding your breath underwater."

"Did the speaker caution everyone not to try this at home?"

"A fair question, Jerry. The talk was a complete disaster. Within just a few minutes, audience members were streaming out of the room. Most of them were holding their noses."

"Were they raising their IQs or commenting on the speech?"

"Take your pick. Back to Flashlight Lady. I can't remember the title of her talk, but she would be doing a series of experiments which would prove that purified food was much better for you than toxic food.

"A whole bunch of people who had just taken the Mensa test had been invited to stay for the rest of the day. Most of them came to her lecture. This would be their first impression of Mensa."

"So, what happened?"

"It was quite an experience. She did a series of quote unquote 'scientific experiments' and she screwed up each one of them. First she showed everyone two glasses of water. One was pure spring water and the other was tap water. So she announced that first she would take a sip of the pure water. She must have gotten the glasses mixed up because right after she took the sip, she spit it, actually spritzed it out. She started coughing and the audience grew alarmed. Finally she recovered enough to inform everyone that she had accidently swallowed the unpurified water."

"What was the audience's reaction?"

"Stunned silence."

"Wow!"

"*Wait!* That's just the beginning. Then she did the toxic grape experiment."

"Where did she get a toxic grape?"

"That was easy, Jerry. She claimed that all grapes are toxic."

"You learn something every day."

"So, she asks for a volunteer—specifically for a 'strong young man.' So this young man— he must have been six foot four—strolled up to the front of the room. She looked at him with a gleam in her eye. And then he asked her, 'You're not going to hurt me, are you?' So the entire crowd cracked up, and even Flashlight Lady was laughing."

"I wish I had been there."

"I'm telling you, it was really great! Then she asks him to hold out both his arms with his palms up. When he does, she announces that she is placing a grape in his left hand and nothing in this right hand.

"So, then she says to everyone that she's going to try to push down his right arm. Oh, I forgot to tell you that she can't pronounce 'R' if it's the first letter of a word. So she asks the guy, "Beddy?" He nods, so she takes hold of his right arm and presses down while announcing, 'You see, I can't pull down his arm. That's because he doesn't have that toxic grape in his right hand.'"

"Makes sense to me. Then she tries to pull down his left arm?"

"Exactly. Again, she asks, "Beddy?" Then she announces that she's going to pull down his left arm, because that's the arm that has been weakened by the toxic grape. But she can't do it. So, she's actually hanging on his arm, but she can't get it to go down. Soon everyone is laughing. They think that this is some kind of comedy act."

"What did she do?"

"She dismissed him and asked for another volunteer."

"Was she able to pull down the next guy's left arm?"

"No! In fact, *none* of her experiments came out right. But it didn't matter. Because everyone thought that it was all intentional. Sort of like the old 'Gong Show.' When she finally finished, the audience gave her a standing ovation."

"Karen, has Mensa ever considered administering some kind of sanity test for new applicants?"

"It does come up, but we've always chosen to stick with the top two percent in intelligence."

"Smart trumps sane."

"Hey, I *like* that! Maybe we can use it as our motto."

3

When the cab pulled up in front of a five-story town house on Lexington Ave, Karen explained that Mensa rented a room there for their lectures and parties. They climbed the stairs and entered a large room on the second floor. The building was owned by some kind of fraternal organization. "They don't bother *us* and we don't bother *them*."

We signed in and paid a small admission fee. Karen assured me that most of the members were quite friendly, and then she wandered off, leaving me on my own. It looked to me like an almost normal party. There were at least a hundred people, most of whom were standing around talking to each other in small groups. I noticed a few other people either reading books or staring into space. And there were Big Mike and Orange Man, each doing his own thing.

Big Mike stood over a huge bowl stuffing fistfuls of potato chips into his mouth. His hands were much larger than his mouth, because some of the chips were falling back into the bowl. No problem. He wasn't going anywhere.

Orange Man was a much more elegant eater. He had arranged several lines of orange M & Ms and was consuming them, one line at a time. I looked around for the Flashlight Lady, but maybe she was someplace where the food was less toxic.

It seemed like a happy group. There were normal looking people and, well, some unusual looking folks. There was a young woman with purple spiked hair and a tongue ring conversing with an older man wearing a navy-blue suit jacket over a yellow and black Mensa tee shirt. He apparently had on the brown pants belonging to another suit, and one of his cuffs was caught in his white sock. Another guy was wearing black leather pants, a white work shirt, a fully stocked tool belt, and he was talking to a guy who looked like he modeled for GQ.

"You're *new!*" A short guy in a business suit was smiling at me. "I'm Tony."

"Glad to meet you, Tony. I'm Jerry. So how could you tell I was new?"

"A simple deduction. I saw you come in with Karen. Then she walked off and you're standing here looking around. And you don't appear to know anyone."

"Are you a philosopher?"

"Close: I work at the post office."

Just then a nice-looking woman joined us. She was Betty. When I told her that I knew Karen, Betty said, "Oh yeah, she's really smart!" With that, the two of them cracked up.

"She *is?*" I asked.

"That was a Mensa joke," explained Tony. We're *all* supposed to be smart."

"But some animals are more equal than others," said Betty.

"*Animal Farm?*" asked Tony

"Right you are!"

Hearing the laughter, a few other people joined us. "So, you're new?" asked a guy named Don.

"Yeah, how did you know?"

"Well, for starters, I saw you talking to *these* guys."

"So, what do *you* do, Jerry?" asked Betty.

"I teach history."

"In high school?" asked another woman.

"No, at City College."

"Wow, you must be smart!" said Tony with a big grin. Everyone chuckled.

"Well, I hate to tell you...."

"You hate to tell us *what?*" asked another woman who had just joined us.

"Let me put it *this* way. Not only am I not in Mensa, and not only do I have the lowest IQ in this room, but I'll bet my IQ is at least 30 or 40 points lower than that of the person with the next lowest IQ. In fact, according to the tests I took in elementary and middle school, it was somewhere in what they called the normal range—say around 100."

Now things were beginning to get interesting. More people gathered around us. Then Betty said, "I'm sure you'd qualify to get into Mensa." Most of the others nodded.

"Do you have a PhD?" asked Don.

"Well, yeah. They won't hire you without one to teach full time at any of the four-year colleges of the City University."

"If you have a PhD, then you're definitely smart enough to get into Mensa," said some guy.

"Not necessarily," said another guy. "What were your scores on the Graduate Records Exam?"

"Mensa no longer accepts those scores," said someone else.

"Yeah," said Betty, "but what if he took them before Mensa stopped accepting those scores?"

"OK, everybody. I neglected to introduce one very salient fact about my PhD." I now had their undivided attention. "You see, I was in a *remedial* PhD program."

They just stared at me. "OK, you all know about remedial reading, writing, and arithmetic courses in colleges, right?"

Everybody had heard of them.

"Those are just elementary and middle school subjects taught in so-called colleges," said one woman. "But a remedial PhD program is an oxymoron."

"What's an oxymoron?" I asked. I waited a few seconds, and then said, "Gotcha!" Everyone laughed—even the woman who introduced the term.

By now almost all the people at the party had joined around us in a huge circle. I saw Karen at the back of the crowd and she was smiling.

"Let me ask everyone here a question. How many of you have PhDs? More than a dozen hands went up. Then one guy announced, "I have a PhD *and* a JD." Another guy piped up, "I have a PhD and two masters." Then a woman said, "I'll raise you: I have a PhD, an MD, *and* an MA."

I waited a few seconds and then asked with a straight face, "How many of you got any of those degrees through a remedial program?"

There was complete silence. "All right, then. Here's my story. I had just graduated from college and wanted to go to graduate school to study history. I had my heart set on going to New York University. But I don't have to tell any of you how much they charge per credit."

They all nodded their heads and smiled.

"Then I heard that I was eligible to join a pilot remedial PhD program at NYU. It was part of a study financed by a large foundation to determine if students with relatively low IQs could master the same work as traditional graduate students. A group of students in the normal IQ range—90 to 110—would be able to attend NYU completely free of charge. We would have one-on-one support from counselors and tutors. And as long as we received passing grades, we could stay in the program."

"And 110 was the cut-off IQ?"

"That's right, Don."

"*Shit!*"

Everyone laughed.

"So, we all went along at our own pace, taking the same courses, writing the same papers, taking the same exams, and meeting all the same requirements as the regular NYU grad students."

"And you guys all went for free?"

"That's correct, Betty."

"What's the catch?"

"No catch, Tony. But we *did* get one big break. When we took a course, we had two years to complete it, if we needed the time."

"Isn't that like the culture fair test that Mensa gives?" asked a woman.

"Hey," I said, "maybe *then* I could pass the Mensa test."

Everyone laughed.

"We took two courses a semester, and if we had more than one incomplete, we had to make them up before we enrolled in additional courses."

"So how long did it take you to complete your degree?" a woman asked.

"Well, it took me eight years to complete my course work, another three years to study for my written and oral exams, and then six more years onto write my dissertation. Do the math."

Everyone laughed.

"You're really not kidding?" asked Don.

"About what?" I deadpanned.

Again, everyone laughed.

Slowly the crowd began to disperse, but I was still surrounded by about a dozen people. They peppered me with questions. "Do they still have that remedial PhD program?" "How dumb do you have to be to get into it?" "If you're in Mensa, does that disqualify you?" "What if kids in elementary school purposely got low IQ scores and took special education classes?"

"Those are excellent questions," I said. "But I'm not smart enough to know the correct answers."

More and more people continued to drift away. The show was over. Karen gave me the high sign and we headed home.

"Well, Jerry, that was quite a performance."

"Thank you, Karen."

"Now I know that there's nothing normal about you, including your IQ."

"Is that so? I always considered myself average."

"Jerry, I *know* your IQ is far from average."

"You do?"

"Yes."

"I'm puzzled about just one thing."

"And what's that, Karen?"

"You're either extremely smart…"

And now we were both laughing.

A NIGHT AT THE DAKOTA

1

Nobody likes "the professor," but he *does* throw great parties. Lots of good-looking yuppies, excellent food, and an open bar.

A distinguished professor of psychology at the City University, he owns a huge apartment in the Dakota, a landmarked building on Central Park West. He never could have afforded it on his salary, but he earns substantial royalties from his pop psychology books. They include such titles as *"Relations that Last Forever, How to Make Great First Impressions;* and *Anger Management for Dummies."*

You would think that the professor would have a great store of personal experience to draw upon, but apparently his social life revolves entirely around his parties. He stands at the door most of the evening, greeting his guests and checking their names on his list. If you are not on the list, then no amount of begging will get you in.

Pushing sixty, the professor is not an attractive man. With a Donald Trump-sized head looming over the scarecrow body of an Ichabod Crane, he's a rather unusual looking dude. On the bright side, he has a ready-made Halloween costume.

2

Caroline and I met at the gym. She's what guys used to call a real looker: fantastic body, angelic face, and Midwestern nice. *Me?* Just another plain Jane from Queens. Or, as I sometimes overhear some men saying, "Nothing special."

Caroline is one among New York's tens of thousands of aspiring actors, few of whom ever progress beyond a handful of unpaid showcase productions. But she does make a nice living doing commercials.

She confided that most of the men she knew were actors—and you know what *that* means.

"They're gay?"

"You betcha!"

"Hey, y'know what, Caroline? Why not come with me to some parties? You'll meet tons of guys—and all of them will be straight."

"How do you know, Holly?"

"Cause they hit on almost every woman they meet."

"Sounds charming!"

It just so happens that this weird professor is hosting a party on Friday night. And get this: He lives in the Dakota."

"*Rosemary's Baby!* John and Yoko! Oh, and Judy Garland, Leonard Bernstein, and Lauren Bacall! You know, Holly, next to being in a Broadway play, I think visiting where all those stars lived would be almost as much of a kick! Heck, I'd go just to see the building!"

3

Three nights later we took a cab across the park and walked into the lobby of the Dakota. The professor had left a list downstairs, and the doorman checked off my name. "And is this beautiful woman with you?"

"She sure is!"

"Here for the first time, honey?"

"Yesiree!"

"Well then, if you'd like, have a look around the lobby before you go upstairs. And if you have any questions, I'm here till midnight."

40

We thanked him and began walking around the lobby. The only thing I knew about the Dakota's history was that it was built in the early 1880s. So I just let Caroline do her tourist thing. As we approached the elevator, we were joined by two empty suits that were also on their way to the party.

Before we'd reached our floor, they were both coming on to Caroline, while completely ignoring me. Caroline introduced me, and very sweetly said that we could all get to know each other much better at the party.

As we exited the elevator, it sounded as though hundreds of people were all talking at the same time. We had to keep banging on the door till it was opened and the professor peered out. He nodded at the two suits, who quickly entered the apartment. He gave me a weak smile, saying "*You* I know!" Then he looked at Caroline.

I knew quite well how men reacted to her so I was expecting some sort of lecherous remark like, "What have we *here?*" *Boy* was I wrong! Without warning, he screamed, "How *dare* you try to sneak into my party? Get *out* of here!"

I could see the veins in his neck swelling. His face went from pasty white to deep purple. He screamed louder and louder. "You goddamn bitch! Slut! Whore!"

He struggled to catch his breath, and was now shouting at the top of his lungs: "You think you can crash my party? Eat my food? Drink my liquor?"

I was afraid he would have a heart attack! I yelled the first thing that popped into my head: "*Professor!* She's with *me!*"

Silence. The color began to drain from his face. The three of us just stood there. Then he opened the door wide and said, "You may both come in."

Caroline and I looked at each other, shrugged, and went inside. He followed us in, locked the door, and then turned to Caroline. "My dear, may I have your telephone number?"

Part II

SEX IN THE CITY

New York was the birthplace of the sexual revolution. After the repressive 1950s, twenty- and thirty-something's acted like kids in a candy store. Such questions as "Getting any?" and "Does she put out?" were still asked only by complete losers. Remember the game, musical chairs? We used beds.

LOOKING FOR LOVE IN ALL THE WRONG PLACES

Back in the 1950s, there was one clear dichotomy in the teenage social world— "good girls" and "bad girls." If you *did* it, you were a bad girl.

And guys? Nearly all of them *wanted* to, but few of them "got lucky."

Johanna was a *very* good girl, but not really out of choice. Somewhat shy, she had a nice smile and an attractive figure. Still, by her eighteenth birthday she had had only three dates. And as luck would have it, the boys were even shyer than *she* was.

Had she ever been kissed? Not really. The only guy who had ever tried was her friend's fifty-year-old drunken uncle, who accosted her at a bar mitzvah. She slapped him so hard, he spilled his drink all over himself. Then she heard his wife yell across the room, "Morris! *Again?*"

Her two best friends, Carmella and Eileen, were not a whole lot more experienced than she was. One evening, the three of them decided that it might be fun to go into the city and do a little bar-hopping. They had heard that a bar was a good place to meet guys.

They went from bar to bar, but none of them even got into a conversation. The guys were either disinterested, or maybe too shy to talk to them.

Just before deciding to call it a night, they looked into the window of a dimly lit bar just off Sheridan Square in Greenwich Village.

"Look Johanna, this place is full of gorgeous guys."

Carmella was right! One guy was better looking than the next. They decided to give this place a shot before they took the subway back to Queens.

Music was blaring from the juke box. Elvis was singing, "Love me tender." A guy came over to Johanna and asked her to dance.

Why *not*? He was quite handsome! His name was Michael.

He pulled her close. She could smell his aftershave lotion. She rested her head on his shoulder.

Where had *this* guy been all her life? Then she *felt* something pressing against her. Oh, my *God!* Could that be what she *thought* it was?

What should she do? Could *she* actually have this effect on a man? And such an *attractive* man? Michael could have *any* woman he wanted. So why did he pick *me*?

She decided to just go with the moment and enjoy it. Maybe *every* woman excited him. Maybe he was some kind of sex fiend.

She laughed to herself. The last way she would have ever described herself would have been as a "sex object." Then she realized the song had ended. They just stood there, their arms around each other.

Another song came on, and they began to dance again. It was Elvis again, this time singing, "Don't be cruel, to a heart that's true."

Elvis could actually sense her hopes, her fears. She wondered if Michael also could. She felt his erection growing, and tried to imagine how big it could possibly get.

Now he was kissing her neck. She began to sigh. Michael knew exactly what he was doing. She couldn't wait to see what he would do next.

A shock went right through her when she felt his tongue dip into her ear. It was all she could do to not scream out. Where had she *been* all these years?

She began to shudder as he went deeper into her ear—in and out, in and out. Then he switched to the other ear.

Soon, very slowly he moved his hands down her back, pausing every few seconds to rub, and finally reaching her butt.

What was he going to do *now*?

He did not make her wait. Placing one hand on each cheek, he began to very tenderly squeeze each of them. She had never dreamed that anyone could touch her this way.

"Don't *stop!* Don't *ever* stop!" she silently begged.

He heard her loud and clear.

She had no idea what he could possibly do next. If he had wanted to take her right there on the floor, she would have *let* him. She would do *any*thing with this man.

She wondered how many women in the world were having done to them what she was having done to *her*. Especially, in a crowded bar with her two best friends nearby. What could they *possibly* be thinking?

For a few seconds she imagined what would happen to her "reputation." She didn't care. The only thing that mattered was what *he* was doing to her.

Just then, she felt him tense up, and a second later there was a shout!

"Michael, you *fucking whore!*"

She felt him being yanked away from her. What was *happening*?

Michael and the other guy squared off and looked like they were going to rush at each other. But quickly, several other guys pulled them apart. Carmella and Eileen rushed over to Johanna.

"Time to go home!" declared Eileen, as she and Carmella hustled Johanna out into the street.

After they had walked a block, Carmella summed it all up.

"Johanna, just in case you didn't notice, that was a *homo* bar!"

"But he... he…"

"Look at it *this* way," said Eileen. "He found you so attractive, he couldn't help himself!"

The three of them began to laugh hysterically. Then Johanna looked at her friends and asked in a mock serious tone, "So I'm still a *good* girl, right?"

THE DINNER TEST

There aren't many guys left on the Upper Westside who haven't been in the sack with "bed-and-breakfast Barbara." And according to Barbara, most of them are either gay or still live with their mothers.

"Look," she tells me, "I'm too young to retire to a convent. Maybe I should move to another neighborhood and start all over again."

"Barbara," I tell her, "it's just going to be the same thing all over again. You know: the dinner test, a roll in the hay, slam-bam, thank you ma' am, see yuh around the quad."

"Don't knock the dinner test, Judy. If a guy can't get through dinner without picking his teeth, forget it!"

"Wasn't there some guy who smacked his lips when he ate? Jerry?"

"Nah, Jerry was the food sprayer. He was just a pig. But Alex was the lip smacker. Judy, he was just unbelievable! Everybody in the restaurant was looking at us. They heard this noise corning from our table. I thought they were going to throw us out of the restaurant."

"Did you sleep with him?"

"Gimme a break, Judy!"

"Who was the guy with the purple knapsack? I think you had a blind date with him."

"That guy didn't even get into the restaurant. I was supposed to meet him outside. Well, I saw this guy walking up the street, a real geek. And check this out, Judy: the guy's picking his nose."

"Charming."

"So, he walks up to me and says, 'Barbara?' I tell him, no, my name is Judy."

"Come on, tell me what you said to him."

"I told him that Barbara couldn't make it. She had to work late and she sent me to give him the bad news."

"Did he buy it?"

"Sure. Then he asked me if I would like to have dinner with him."

"*Did* you?"

"Are you *nuts!* I told him I had to go back to work myself, and I left him standing there."

"Did he call you after that?"

"Every day for about a month. Thank God for answering machines."

"Maybe that guy would have passed the dinner test."

"Yeah, right! Then I could have found out what he was carrying in that knapsack."

"So, Barbara, a guy passes the dinner test if he doesn't spray his food, smack his lips, pick his nose or his teeth."

"Actually, those are just for starters. There was one guy who picked me up at work. As we were driving to the restaurant, he puts his hand on my thigh.

"What did you do?"

"I told him to stop the car because I had to puke. I got out, left the door open, and started walking."

"What a presumptuous jerk!"

"Then there was the guy who tried to beat the check by running out of the restaurant. He whispers to me, 'Barbara, run for it!'"

"*Did* you?"

"Are you *kidding*? I told him that if he didn't pay, I'd give his name and address to the manager."

"I can't believe he did that to you. Maybe he thought *you* would pay."

"Get *real*, Judy! I never paid for a date in my life. The guy pays. And that, by the way, is the main part of the dinner test."

"Did any guys ask you to pay?"

"No, but I had a couple of nerds who suggested that we go Dutch."

"Get *out*!"

"Can you *believe* it, Judy? What do they think? That this is still the seventies with all that women's lib crap? The guy takes the woman out. He pays. End of discussion."

"OK, Barbara, you go out with a guy. He doesn't do anything disgusting over dinner. He doesn't have a purple knapsack. He pays the check. So, then you go to bed with him?"

"Right."

"What if you're not attracted to him?"

"I only go out with guys I'm attracted to. Unless he's a blind date. And if he turns out to be a dork like the guy with the knapsack, I don't go through with it."

"OK, these guys who passed the dinner test—you went to bed with all of them on that first date?"

"Right."

"And *then* what?"

"Well, Judy, some of them I never heard from again. Some of them I saw maybe once or twice."

"*Then* what happened?"

"Oh, I don't know. I got sick of them. They got sick of me."

"But that thing you had going with Marty? How long did *that* last?"

"Too long! Much too long. The guy was too perfect. He held doors for me, took me to expensive places, brought me flowers, and he even started making noises about getting engaged."

"So why *didn't* you, Barbara?"

"I already told you. Marty was *too* perfect. There was no excitement. No surprises. Even the sex."

"You mean like it was a routine?"

"Worse. For some reason we'd see each other on weekends and Wednesday night. Why I don't know. And we'd have sex once on Friday night and once on Saturday night, but never on Wednesday."

"You mean like that old movie?"

"Yeah. Come to think of it, never on Sunday either."

"Why not?"

"Well, Marty had this theory about girls. They'd be very upset if a guy slept with them and then didn't spend the night. And Marty didn't stay over on Sunday night or Wednesday night."

"Why not?"

"Because Mondays and Thursdays were workdays."

"Well, Barbara, just think of what it would have been like being married to him. You'd end up having sex just on weekends."

"Yeah, and the night before holidays."

"Wasn't there anyone else you got involved with besides Marty?"

"Well, there was Gary, who was the love of my life."

"I don't remember you ever mentioning him. Was he a while back?"

"Ages ago. Right after I moved to this apartment. Gary was great. Great looking. Great in bed. Fun. Exciting."

"And not just on Friday and Saturday night?"

"Gary was like, let's do it, whenever, wherever. Once we were at my aunt's apartment and she went into the bedroom to take a phone call. Gary laid me out right on the living room couch. Believe it not, first time we ever did it. While my aunt was talking on the phone."

"Was it exciting that she could have walked in on you?"

"It was unbelievable! You should try it sometime."

"So why did you and Gary break up?"

"You're not going to believe this! We had been seeing each other for about four months. Weekdays, weekends, we'd go on trips—everything. Then I found out that not only was the bastard married, but he had another girlfriend on the side. And the wife, the other girlfriend and I each thought we had an exclusive."

"How did he get away with it? *And* keep three women happy at the same time!"

"I'll give him that. Gary was quite the stud."

"Barbara, do you think you'll ever meet anyone?"

"Who knows? I'm still having fun. And I'm always open to new experiences."

"Oh yeah? There's a cute guy I know from work. Shall we set him up for a dinner test?"

"Sure, why not?"

"Shall I describe him?"

"Just tell me one thing, Judy. What color is his knapsack?"

DEAR ABBY

Dear Abby was the most widely read and longest running advice column ever written. Here are excerpts from five recently discovered columns from the late 1960s. All were written in response to questions from New Yorkers who found themselves on the cutting edge of the Sexual Revolution.

DEAR ABBEY:
A woman never pays on a date? Right? That's the way I was brought up. So let me ask you: On a date, should a woman ever agree to go Dutch?
DEAR DUTCH-TREATER:
Only if she has no intention of sleeping with her date. These are the sixties, honey! Better to be known as a "sleep-around" than a "gold-digger." No one respects a gold-digger.

DEAR ABBY:
Is a girl who goes to a guy's house for dinner obligated to sleep with him?
DEAR DINNER GUEST:
Are you going there for the cooking? Seriously, sweetie, if you aren't, you'll certainly make a bad impression.

DEAR ABBY:
Over the last few weeks I've had three women over for dinner. But none of them slept with me. What should I do to get better results?

DEAR COOK:

You must be quite a cook! My advice: Don't feed them until they've paid for their meal.

DEAR ABBY:

I've gone out with this guy a couple of times, but I'm not that attracted to him. When should I sleep with him?

DEAR NOT-THAT-ATTRACTED:

You have been leading him on. Etiquette dictates that a woman should sleep with a man by the second date. If not, you'll get a bad reputation.

DEAR ABBY:

I'm sleeping with four different women. Is there anything *wrong* with that?

DEAR ROMEO:

Wrong with *what*?

MR. SENSITIVITY

1

I like to think that I'm a pretty sensitive guy, but why don't *you* be the judge? I'll tell you about some stuff that happened to me and let you draw your own conclusions.

You're familiar with Psoriasis, the dry, crusty skin condition? Although a lot of people have it, it's usually pretty mild. But if you have a bad case, it can really fuck up your life.

Nick was not someone I would have typically chosen to be friends with. He *was* very good looking, and you could see that he worked out. But he rarely smiled, almost never spoke, and appeared to have no personality.

He always wore long sleeve shirts, even in the summer. But I caught glimpses of his wrists and quickly realized that he must have had a very bad case of psoriasis.

I knew Nick through my good buddy, Matt. Nick was usually with his girlfriend, Carla, who was almost his exact opposite—sweet, friendly, and very homely. She seemed quite happy with him. Perhaps there really *is* someone for everyone. You overlook *my* problems, and I overlook *yours*.

Then, I heard from Matt that Nick and Carla had broken up. I thought to myself: How will that poor guy ever find another girlfriend?

Matt must have read my mind. "Do you *know* anyone for Nick? That poor bastard really needs to get himself laid."

Matt must have realized that I was aware of Nick's medical problem, though he never mentioned it. We both knew that finding someone for Nick would not be easy. I doubted that I could think of anyone.

2

I thought about how hard it must be for Nick. Who would even go out with him, let alone go to bed with him? I wondered if Nick had taken off his shirt when he did it with Carla. Or if they even talked about his Psoriasis.

I tried to think of a personal ad that Nick could place in some magazine: "Good looking guy with no personality and slight skin condition needs someone to fuck." No, too subtle.

How about, "If you like good-looking guys with bad cases of Psoriasis, I'm your man"?

Maybe *I* should take out an ad for Nick, and see if anyone responded. I wondered if there were places to find women with terrible self-images, who might like Nick. Prisons? Insane asylums?

Then I thought of a woman who just might be willing to overlook Nick's problem. Of course, she was a little bit nuts, but I mean that in a *good* way.

Millie would call me from time to time and coyly ask, "Do you want company?"

And I'd say, "Sure, come on over."

She'd come by, take off her clothes, and then say, "I want you to hurt me."

I took that to mean that she wanted me to fuck her hard, so I would oblige. Soon she'd be digging her nails into my back and screaming, "Don't *stop*! Don't fucking *stop!*"

When she was ready to leave, which was usually pretty late at night, she'd ask me to walk her to the subway. This was, of course, the least I could do.

One evening, as we climbed into bed, she whispered, "I want you to *really* hurt me!"

This somehow made me smile. I'm not really into any of that S & M shit, so I asked, "Do you want me to punch you in the nose?"

"No! I want you to *spank* me!"

Well that I can handle, so to speak. So she lay across my lap and I spanked her.

"Harder!" she demanded.

So, I spanked harder.

"Is *that* the best you can do?" she yelled.

Now I happen to be a pretty strong guy, but I didn't want to hurt her.

I spanked her a little harder. She began to shudder. Then she rolled off me onto the bed and demanded, "Now fuck me hard up the ass!"

I did as I was told.

3

I wasn't all that crazy about Millie, and I knew that she was not particularly fond of me. We treated each other like appliances that could be ignored until the next time they were needed. I mean, I wouldn't want anything *bad* to happen to her, but I almost never thought about her until her next phone call. And she seemed to have absolutely no curiosity about *my* life.

A few days after Matt's call, it suddenly *hit* me: Millie would be perfect for Nick!

I got Nick's number from Matt and called him. When I began telling him about Millie, he grew very interested. He seemed to like women who wanted a guy to hurt them.

I knew that I needed to handle the next step very carefully. I could not even allude to his skin condition, and yet I wanted him to think that she would be willing to overlook it. Not that I was that sure she *would* be.

"Nick, I need to tell you something about her. And this might turn you off. She wants you to fuck her very hard."

"No problem."

"Yeah, but when *I* did, she dug her nails into my back. And I have the scars to prove it."

Nick didn't say anything. I knew he was thinking.

"So Nick, I came up with a great solution."

"Yeah?"

"I wouldn't take off my shirt when we went to bed."

"*Really?*"

"Yeah, and it worked!"

Nick happily took down Millie's number, and even thanked me for it.

Say, did I mention that the guy had virtually no personality? I hoped the two of them would be very happy together.

4

Matt and I were pretty tight friends. We had the keys to each other's apartments. He stayed at his grandmother's in the Baruch Houses—a public housing project just a few blocks from me. I lived in an old apartment building near Delancey and Essex. If you're familiar with that corner of Manhattan, you know that I'm talking about the Lower East Side. Back in the early 1970s, it was still a slum.

Matt's grandmother lived in Florida for half the year, so occasionally he had parties in the apartment. And every so often, when his grandmother was around, he used my place to get laid. When I got home late one evening I found a short note taped to my bedroom door. Above his signature were eight "x" marks.

After Nick and Millie began seeing each other, Matt decided to throw a party. Millie had fixed him up on a blind date with her friend, Trudy, who lived in Canarsie, which was way out in Brooklyn. She wanted Matt to pick her up. He would have to take two trains and a bus to get to her house.

I had a date that night with a woman I had just met, and she lived on Staten Island. And *that* required taking a bus to the ferry, and then another bus to her house. She promised to make the trip well worth my while.

It took me almost two hours to get to her house, ostensibly to meet her parents. They weren't home, but she expected them any minute. And then we could leave for the party.

While we were waiting, one thing led to another. To make a short story even shorter, she definitely kept her word about making my trip worthwhile. She later confessed that her parents would not be getting home until early the next morning.

By then we had missed the last ferry. I didn't bother calling Matt to tell him that we couldn't make it.

5

Meanwhile, Matt had arrived at his date's house, and the two of them made their way back to the party. They arrived just before midnight.

As soon as they walked in, Matt asked Nick, "Where the fuck is Steve?"

"How the hell should *I* know?"

Matt was incredulous. "He didn't call?"

Nick and Millie both shook their heads "no."

"Did you at least *hear* the fuckin' phone ring during the last five hours?"

No, they hadn't.

So Matt declared the party over. As he and his date walked to the door, he yelled, "I want the two of you to be here when I get back!"

6

We knew it would not be such a great idea for me to be there when her parents got home, so she called a car service, and I was on the five o'clock ferry to Manhattan.

When I finally got home, it was getting light. I felt guilty as hell, but Matt's party was a pretty stupid idea to begin with. I hoped that somehow his date worked out as well as mine had.

The first thing I did was take the phone off the hook. I figured that Matt might try reaching me, but I had had almost no sleep—not that I was complaining.

I threw off my clothes, pulled the covers over my head, and must have immediately fallen asleep. I awoke to the sound of voices in the apartment. Matt's growl was very easy to recognize. Then I heard someone laughing. That must have been Nick. And there was a woman's voice. She seemed to be complaining about something. I thought I heard her saying something like, "No, I won't *do* it!"

I was wide awake as the three of them came stomping into my bedroom. Matt started pulling the covers off me. I always sleep naked, and I instinctively tried to keep myself covered. Of course, that was ludicrous, since this entire charade was being staged to embarrass me in front of Millie.

But Matt and Nick both knew she had seen me naked many times before now. So why this whole performance? Only Matt could know for sure.

Then it dawned on me that we had all been assigned parts to play. Millie was the innocent young woman who was forced to witness this lewd display. Nick had a more subtle role. He had to affirm Millie's innocence—and then too, his own. He would have been just as shocked to learn that Millie and I had ever *done* anything.

And Matt? He was the playwright, producer, director, *and* the leading man.

Millie was great! Despite Nick's best efforts, he couldn't pry her hands from her eyes. "*No!* I *won't!* I *won't!*

Then Matt snarled, "Nick, help me pull off this fucking blanket!"

I hung on for dear life, but with the two of them yanking from both ends, I figured it was better to let go before they wrecked my bed.

It was all over as quickly as it had begun. Matt and Nick marched out of the apartment, with Millie in their wake. They left the door wide open, so I would have to get up to lock it.

THE PHONE CALL

CHRISTINA   Hello, is this Mark?

MARK   Yes, who's this?

CHRISTINA   Christina.

MARK   Christina?

CHRISTINA   Yes, but you don't know me.

MARK   Then why are you calling?

CHRISTINA   OK. Now this is going to seem crazy to you. I was having dinner with this guy last night. And he was talking about you.

MARK   What's his name?

CHRISTINA   Dennis Woodson.

MARK   I don't know him.

CHRISTINA   I know. But his cousin knows this woman?

MARK   Yeah?

CHRISTINA   Norma? Or Nora?

MARK   Why are you calling me? Who *are* you?

CHRISTINA   I wanted to ask you a question. About what Dennis said about you last night?

MARK   I don't want to answer any questions. I don't even want to *ask* any questions.

CHRISTINA   (In little girl voice) *Please*, Mark. I really had to get up the courage to call you. I thought about you all last night. And I got up real

	early this morning, trying to get up my nerve. But I was afraid you might be mad.
MARK	Don't worry, I'm not mad.
CHRISTINA	Will you answer my question?
MARK	Maybe. Let me hear the question.
CHRISTINA	I'm embarrassed.
MARK	Oh, come on—it can't be all that bad.
CHRISTINA	I'm afraid. You won't get *mad* at me?
MARK	No, Christina. I promise.
CHRISTINA	Are you ready? OK. Do you like women to make doody in your mouth?
MARK	WHAT? Are you CRAZY! I never *did* that! Never! Never! Well, maybe *once*. Almost.
CHRISTINA	Really?
MARK	OK! OK! Twice! Years ago. Fifteen *years* ago.
CHRISTINA	Did she actually do it right into your mouth?
MARK	No! No! Maybe just a fart. Or just a little piece. It was nothing— nothing at all.
CHRISTINA	Did you spit it out? Or swallow it?
MARK	Are you *crazy*? Of course I spit it out!
CHRISTINA	*All* of it?
MARK	I don't know! Why are you *asking* me this? This all happened fifteen years ago. How do you expect me to remember?
CHRISTINA	Did she actually squat down and do it right in your mouth?
MARK	No—of course not! What do you *think*? No—it wasn't like that at all. In fact it was all very innocent. Very innocent. All I was doing was licking her asshole.
CHRISTINA	You mean Anal Lingus.

MARK	That's right. I'm surprised you know that term. So I was doing Anal-Lyngis on her and she was doing me at the same time. Then I told her to let go. So she tried to, but it was only a fart.
CHRISTINA	Or maybe just a very tiny piece.
MARK	Yeah.
CHRISTINA	So no one can really say that you want a woman to shit in your mouth.
MARK	No, of course not. Look, these things get blown way out of proportion. Just the other day a guy inadvertently touched my cock in a crowded subway train. But I didn't make a big deal out of it. These things happen all the time. I'm sure it was an accident. Anyway, I got off at the next stop, so nothing else happened.
CHRISTINA	I'm sorry to change the subject, but didn't Hitler like women to shit in his mouth?
MARK	*No! No!* It never happened! I'm sure of that! Look there are some people out there spreading rumors that are very unfair to Hitler!
CHRISTINA	Did you want to *do* it with the guy who *inadvertently* touched your cock in the subway?
MARK	No! Of *course* not! What do you take me for?
CHRISTINA	You seem like a nice guy.
MARK	Really? Thank you. You know, you have a very nice voice. And you seem very sweet.
CHRISTINA	Do you think so?

MARK	Let's meet! It was fate that you called me. I was sitting here thinking about how lonely I was, when the phone rang.
CHRISTINA	You don't want to go out with me. You hardly know me. I could be some sort of *per*vert.
MARK	*Really?*
CHRISTINA	No, Mark. I'm really very inhibited. I hope I haven't misled you by asking you such intimate things.
MARK	Well, to tell you the truth, you got me a little worried when you called. Remember you said you wanted to ask me a question?
CHRISTINA	Yeah?
MARK	Well, I thought you were going to ask me something really bad.
CHRISTINA	*This* wasn't bad?
MARK	No—not at all. Tell me, Christina, do *you* have any sexual fantasies.
CHRISTINA	No, I told you, I'm very straight.
MARK	You must! Everybody has them! Fantasies! Everybody has sexual fantasies. *I* have them!
CHRISTINA	Tell me one.
MARK	Do you really want to hear?
CHRISTINA	I'd love to.
MARK	What I'd really like to do—if it was the right person, of course. Are you ready?
CHRISTINA	Uh huh.
MARK	I'd like to lick a nice hairy pair of balls.
CHRISTINA	Are you *gay?*

MARK	Gay! Are you *crazy* or something! Gay? What do you take me for? I'm as straight as they come.
CHRISTINA	But you just said—
MARK	I know what I said! You asked me for a fantasy. That's mine! But it's only a fantasy. I've never actually *done* it. And as long as you don't actually *do* it—
CHRISTINA	Lick a guy's balls?
MARK	Right! As long as you don't lick a guy's balls, then you are not gay.
CHRISTINA	I'm sure you are a strongly heterosexual man.
MARK	Thank you. Really. I don't want you to think there is anything wrong with me. I'm perfectly normal.
CHRISTINA	I know, Mark. I never said you weren't.
MARK	No, but sometimes people take things the wrong way.
CHRISTINA	Do you think *Hitler* was normal?
MARK	Sexually?
CHRISTINA	Yes.
MARK	I don't want to judge him. Personally I think he was pretty straight. Maybe he liked a little kinky stuff, now and then, but what's wrong with that?
CHRISTINA	Nothing.
MARK	So then he was probably normal.
CHRISTINA	Like you?
MARK	Absolutely, I *know* I'm normal. Hitler? Probably. You know how rumors get spread and exaggerated.

CHRISTINA	You're right. That's why I called you. I wanted to hear your side of the story.
MARK	That was decent of you. Not many people would check out their facts.
CHRISTINA	Thank you, Mark. I've got to go now.
MARK	Wait! Don't you want to meet me?
CHRISTINA	I'll tell you what. I'll call you again a few days.
MARK	Why wait? Let's get together today.
CHRISTINA	I can't, Mark. I just hate to rush into these things. But I'll call you in a few days.
MARK	Promise?
CHRISTINA	Promise. After all, it's not every day that I get a chance to talk to a man like you.

THE V.D. CLINIC

"Can I talk to you, Mike? I mean, alone?"

"Sure, Joanie. What's up?"

"What's up is I want to sleep with you."

"*Shit!*"

"Thanks a lot, Mike. I really needed that. You've made my day."

"I'm sorry, Joanie. I'm just a little jumpy is all. About sex, I mean."

'Whatsa matter, big boy? I thought you were a real stud. Anything you want to talk about?"

"OK, you asked for it. Do you want to hear about my days at the V.D. clinic?"

"Gross!"

"You wanna hear?"

"Oh, please, Mike. Please tell me about your days at the V.D. clinic. It's what every woman dreams about from the man she's just propositioned."

"Your sarcastic wit is exceeded only by your inquiring mind."

"Thank you for noticing. Now you may proceed with your story."

"It was a dark and stormy morning. I woke up, went to take a leak, and then, just as I started to pee—God! I thought I was going to die! My cock was burning.

"I didn't know what was *wrong* with me, but my first thought was that I'd never be able to fuck again. And my second thought was that I'd never be able to pee again."

"Poor baby. So how do you know it was V.D.?"

"I didn't right then. I crawled back into bed and pulled the covers over my head. I just lay there, moaning and groaning."

"It still hurt?"

"No, the pain went away after I finished peeing. But I knew that whatever was wrong with me wasn't going to go away. I thought about all those girls I had gone to bed with."

"*That* must have taken some time."

"Funny. You laugh while I'm lying there near death."

"I thought the pain went away?"

"Sure, but I knew that the next time I peed, it would return with a vengeance. I considered not drinking anything. But then I'd get dehydrated. So I'd have to come up with a new plan. A plan of action. I knew I had *some*thing. Some kind of sickness. A disease.

"Then I remembered my health ed course in college. Just about the only course that taught you anything practical. I remembered the test for clap—you know, gonorrhea? You check for discharge.

"Right after we learned that in health ed, a whole bunch of us went down the hall to the men's room and took out our cocks and checked for discharges."

"Sounds quite elegant."

"Oh, you should have been there, Joanie. Thirty guys with their peckers out, squeezing them up and down. Here's the official technique. You take your thumb, forefinger, and middle finger and press the penis gently at its base, trapping any fluid that might be in the column in between the base and the head. Then, very slowly, you slide your fingers alongside the column up to the head of the penis. If a sticky white fluid emerges, you have the clap."

"Or, in many cases, you've just jerked yourself off."

"Wrong! Wrong! Wrong! Jerking off is an entirely different operation, involving all five fingers as well as the palm."

"Would you care to demonstrate?"

"Not just now. We were concluding the test for gonorrhea. In fact, it was back then—not when I actually may have *had* V.D.—but when I took health ed, that we learned about the Wasserman test."

"For syphilis?"

"Oh, so you've received a liberal education, too"

"Very liberal."

"So, you've indicated. Now, back to our story. The Wasserman test. In health ed they told us all about the wonders of syphilis. The lesions. And how it eventually went to your brain, drove you crazy, and finally killed you."

"I've been thinking, Mike. Perhaps that may explain your behavior."

"Thank you very much! You sure know how to flatter a guy."

"My mother taught me."

"I'll bet she did. Anyway, the test for gonorrhea was easy. But to test for syphilis, you need to go to a doctor, which meant the family doctor. 'Excuse me, Dr. Bernstein, could I have a blood test?' 'Are you getting married, Mike?' 'No, I just thought I'd like to have a Wasserman.' 'I see. Is there anything *else* you'd like to discuss?' 'Yeah, doctor, I've had lesions for a while on my penis and I thought it might be a good idea to have a Wasserman test.' 'Good idea, Mike. We'll just take a little sample of your blood and I'll have the lab run the test.'"

"So, what does all this have to do with that time you couldn't pee?"

"Nothing directly. But it's all somehow tied together. Anyway, right after we learned about venereal diseases, a bunch of us were looking for a clubhouse—really a basement—where we could hold parties. We went to one house that advertised and the woman took us downstairs. She had a lovely furnished basement. The price was right and the location was great. There was only one problem… her name."

"Here name?"

"Yeah, her name was Mrs. Wasserman. As soon as she told us, most of us just broke up. She must have been insulted because she threw us out of there. And a couple of the guys took it as some kind of omen. *She* knew."

"*What* did she know?"

"She knew we were a bunch of syphilitics. Anyone with that name *had* to know. We knew she knew. She knew we knew she knew. She had to throw us out of there. The woman had no choice."

"Enough of Mrs. Wasserman. We're still back there that morning when you couldn't pee."

"Right! So, I was lying there with the covers over my head, moaning and groaning. And then, suddenly I *had* it. I turned on the light, took my thumb, forefinger, and middle finger and placed them at the base of my penis."

"You had the sticky white fluid."

"I had the sticky white fluid."

"So, you went to the V.D. clinic. Why didn't you go to your private doctor?"

"I couldn't go to Dr. Bernstein. What if he told my parents?"

"Do you mean to tell me that a thirty-year-old man was worried that his family doctor would inform his parents that their son had gonorrhea?"

"What can I say? Jewish guys mature late."

"*Tell* me about it!"

"So, I had no alternative but to go to the V.D. clinic. You ever been there?"

"No, I'm forced to admit that I've never had the pleasure."

"Let me describe it. I walked in and everyone was sitting on these dark green iron benches. The walls were green. Dark green from the floor up to about the four feet mark, and then light green up to the ceiling. The floor had green linoleum."

"And I bet *you* were green."

"Probably. So, when I walked in, all these guys looked up at me and smiled."

"They *knew* you?"

74

"No, they were just smiling because they knew why I was there."

"Wasn't that why *they* were there?"

"Yeah, so after I figured that out, I noticed that they looked away from me and back down at the green linoleum. Until the next guy came in."

"Weren't there any women in there?"

"No, the women went to a different clinic on the other side of the building."

"Wouldn't it have been a better idea to integrate the clinics? After all, you couldn't catch anything you didn't already have."

"You laugh, Joanie! But I'll tell you something. I had this friend, Jerry. Jerry was the horniest guy going. Always trying to get laid. In fact we used to say that Jerry's motto was—if it moves, *fuck* it.

"So, Jerry gets this idea one day. He's going to stand outside the women's clinic and try to pick up women coming out of there. He figured that by hitting on promiscuous women, he'd increase his odds of scoring."

"He'd increase his chance of getting V.D. God, what did this Jerry *look* like?"

"Funny you should ask. He was this scraggly little fellow, who acted kind of crazy. He was always on unemployment and he never had his own apartment. He often house sat for people. And when he talked to you, he would look at you with his left eye. His right eye seemed to be focused off somewhere in the distance. But his most prominent feature was those lesions he had all over his cock."

"Ha! Ha! Hardy *ha!* You can't be serious for a minute."

"Why, do you want to meet him? I think I might be able to arrange an introduction."

"No, one pervert at a time is quite enough."

"How can you possibly call me a pervert? You didn't even find out yet whether I had the clap."

"Well, *did* you?"

"I'm getting to that. First, I have to tell you what happened at the clinic. They gave me a number and told me to sit on a bench. After about half an hour they told about ten of us to form a line in numerical order. I think I was number 224."

"Busy day."

"Well, it was kind of nice to know that I wasn't the only one who woke up and thought his cock was on fire. Misery sure had a lot of company *that* morning!"

"Come *on*, already! Did you *have* it?"

"Patience. After all, I was the one with the burning cock.

"So, I'm number 224. Number 223 was this big hippie. He must have been six foot eight and had to weigh a good 380 pounds. I mean he was *big!*"

"How big *was* he?"

"He was so big that he had a bench all to himself. He was so big that when he walked, everything in the room vibrated. And what I remember the most about him was his head. It was gigantic. He had this short, very curly black hair. He looked like someone wearing a buffalo's head."

"Did you see his penis?"

"As a matter a fact I did."

"And was it...?" She separates her palms by about two feet.

"No, actually it was surprisingly small."

"How big were his hands?"

"His hands were huge. Did you ever see those basketball players palm a basketball in each hand? Well, this guy could palm probably two huge *beach* balls.

"Now don't tell me: you really think there's a correlation between the size of a guy's hands and his cock?"

"Don't *you?*"

"Well, no, actually I don't."

"Then you must have a big one."

"Because I have small hands?"

"Yeah, and because you don't think there is a correlation."

"OK, *enough!* The guy had big hands and a small cock. But the best was yet to come, so to speak. The doctor was sitting there with a box of Q-tips and a stack of slides. And he'd work us assembly line fashion. 'Number 221. Drop your pants. Milk it.'

"Then the doctor got some of the sticky white discharge on the Q-tip and swabbed it on the slide. 'Number 222. Drop your pants.'"

"You were 224?"

"Yeah. But that big hippie was in front of me. I had to stand ten feet off to the side to see what was going on.

"Then it was the big guy's turn. 'Number 223. Drop your pants. Milk it.'

"Something was wrong! 'Keep milking it.' But nothing was coming out. So the doctor pushed the Q-tip into the poor guy's cock. And the guy started screaming! Bellowing! The whole place shook. And everybody started laughing. Guys were doubling over in hysterics. Funniest thing they ever saw.

"And the big hippie went hopping out of there, trying to yank up his pants. We could hear him screaming all the way down the block."

"You were laughing too?"

"I was at first. Then I realized that I was next. 'Number 224. Drop your pants. Milk it.' I closed my eyes and prayed for a discharge. 'Please God, give me gonorrhea if I don't already have it.' I felt the tip of the Q-tip. And then I heard the words I wanted to hear more than any other words in the world.

"'Number 225. Drop you pants.'"

"Did you have gonorrhea?"

"Hold it there a second—not so fast. They still needed to grow a culture to determine the discharge was indeed gonorrhea."

"What else could it have been?"

"I don't know. A vaginal infection?"

"Very cute, Mike. So when did you find out?"

"Oh, I found out about a week later. But before I left the clinic, they gave me a shot of penicillin since nearly everyone *did* turn out to have the clap. And then I got to meet the V.D. investigator."

"Did he ask you a lot of questions? Who you slept with in the last few weeks? Boy, it must have been quite a list."

"No, actually I gave him just one name. Yours."

"Suave. Very suave, Mike. So did you have gonorrhea or not?"

"You really want to know? I mean, do you *really* want to know? The envelope, please. Thank you. The answer is…'yes!'"

"You probably got it by praying for that discharge."

"Believe me, it would have been well worth it."

"Are you cured?"

"Of course I'm cured. I must have taken penicillin four times a day for a week. And believe me, if I wasn't cured, I'd *know* it."

"And so would all your girlfriends."

"Well, it just so happens that right now, there is just one."

"One! I can't believe my ears! Michael Kaplan, the stud of the City?"

"That's right, Joanie. And for now, at least, you're the one."

"Why *me*?"

"Who else would have believed that story about the V.D. clinic?"

NEED A DATE?

1

I'm gonna be honest with yuh, OK? A lotta guys lie about their age, and if there's one thing I hate, it's a liar. I'm pushin' fifty. That's right—the big five-oh.

Yuh don't believe me? Yuh wanna see my driver's license? OK already! It says fifty-three. Yuh can't lie tuh Motor Vehicle or they'll take away yer license.

So, duh yuh need a date? Because I happen tuh run a dating service. It's very sophisticated, very discreet. I only take the most refined clients. No one hasta know I'm gettin' paid tuh go out with a lady. Even *yuh*!

I know yuh must be wondering—how can that be? Am I *right*? So, I'll tell yuh. I'll give yuh an actual example.

2

One day this lady calls me and says she wants tuh fix me up with her niece. The poor girl had just gone through a very bad divorce, so could I pretend I was dating her?

"Fine," I said. "I'm a good actor." But in this case, I would be a little *too* good.

The niece turned out tuh be this plain Jane, if yuh follow what I'm tellin' yuh. I mean, I wouldn't throw her outta bed or anything. But on the other hand, she wasn't no Playboy bunny, neither.

So I go pick her up on this date, and as soon as she gets in my car, she's all over me. Well, we're making out like crazy, and soon she sez, "Duh yuh think we could *go* someplace?"

Well, before I tell yuh what happens, I'm gonna level with yuh. I run a completely legit outfit. This ain't no male prostitution ring.

So, I take her back tuh *my* place, and we go at it all night. Lemme *tell* yuh, it was the easiest money I ever made. It turns out the aunt was loaded, so when I told her that these services were extra, she just doubled my hourly rate.

Well, soon we're seein' each other twice a week, and then three times a week. Between her payin' the babysitter and the aunt payin' me, I figured the president should give me a medal for this economic stimulus package.

But things started gettin' a little hairy. The girl—OK, she was on the wrong side of forty—she tells me she's in love with me.

Shit!

So I tell the aunt. She thinks about it for a minute, and then she says I better break if off. She didn't want me to break her niece's heart.

OK, I tell her. I call the girl, and when I give her the bad news, she starts crying. I felt like a complete piece of shit. I mean, if it wasn't for the money, I'd never ever have done something like that to a girl I was dating. I had this friend, Eddie, who used tuh say, "Don't start up with a girl unless you want tuh keep seein' her."

There's no way I'd ever have gotten involved with a girl like that, but a job's a job. She was nice an all, but she wasn't exactly a looker, if yuh get what I mean. So, am I right or wrong?

Anyway, I was a little sad for a day or two. Then an envelope arrived from the aunt. It made me feel a whole lot better.

3

Business was so good I hired my friend, Jimmy, who I knew from high school. A retired policeman, he was looking to pick up a few bucks.

One day I got a call from what sounded like a rather old lady. She wanted a young man who would "go."

"Go where?" I asked myself. Then I guessed she must have meant go to bed. I explained that anything that happened between her and her date would be OK, but I could not discuss that over the phone. That seemed to satisfy her because she started to cackle. Then, just before hanging up, she said, "Whatever."

I told Jimmy about the call and he seemed game. I gave him the address and he went there a few hours later. It was to be a dinner date at her apartment, which happened to be on Park Avenue in the sixties. Not too shabby.

When Jimmy rang the bell, a uniformed servant about Jimmy's age opened the door, and then led him down a long hallway and into a huge dining room. There were two place settings at either end of a twenty-foot table. After Jimmy was seated, the servant asked if he would like a cocktail.

Two minutes later, Jimmy had his Dewar's on the rocks.

"Will there be anything else, sir?"

"Yes. I was curious about what we would be having for dinner."

"Would prime rib be satisfactory?"

"Most satisfactory! Could I have it medium rare?"

"Of course! There will also be a salad, dinner rolls, and a baked potato."

"Excellent!"

The servant went back into the kitchen and returned with another drink, which he placed at the other end of the table.

A minute later she made her entrance. She leaned on a walker and seemed not to notice Jimmy until she had been seated.

"I'm so glad you could join me, young man. My name is Martha."

"I've very happy to be here, Martha. My name is Jimmy."

81

"Well Jimmy, you look very nice. And I hope you have a very pleasant evening."

"Thank you."

Then she lifted what appeared to be a small radio to her ear and seemed to listen attentively. After several minutes she looked up, and seemed almost surprised to see Jimmy. She smiled at him and confided that they were expecting rain tomorrow.

Just then the servant came back to announce, "Dinner is served."

The prime rib was excellent, as was the rest of the meal. Jimmy wasn't sure what his dinner companion was eating, but she seemed much more absorbed by the weather than by whatever it was that she was spooning down.

And then she stood, bid him good night, and made her way out of the room. The servant came back, handed Jimmy an envelope, and asked if they could talk for a few minutes.

"Of course!"

He sat a couple of seats down from Jimmy. He apologized for anything Mrs. Charles might have said to him. It turned out that she called dating services two or three times a week, and sometimes said some rather crude things.

"Yes, I've heard something to that effect."

"Well, I just wish my mother..."

"Your *mother?*"

Jimmy now realized that he had been taken in by their whole charade.

"Jimmy, I am so *embarrassed!*"

"Tell me...."

"George."

"Tell me, George. Why do you go along with this craziness?"

"Well, she just loves this role playing. She gets a big kick out of having me dress up like a butler."

"And what's with the radio?"

"It has just one station—and all it has are constantly updated weather reports."

"*That's* strange!"

"You want *strange?* My mother has not left the house in nearly twenty years."

Jimmy was thinking that if he had an apartment like this, maybe he wouldn't leave either.

4

Have yuh been wondering how much of a market there is for this kind of business? Yuh know the old saying, "There's someone for everyone"?

Well, I hate to be the one tuh bring yuh the bad news, but that just ain't true for older women lookin' for someone tuh date. That's because of a simple fact: women live longer than men.

In other words, the guys they would've dated are already dead. So, what fun would *they* be?

So why not turn a *bad* thing into a *good* thing? Instead of trying to find men who aren't already dead, get yuhself a younger guy—a guy like me or Jimmy. *Trust* me, yuh could do a lot worse.

Anyway, my phone is ringing off the hook, so I'm looking to hire at least one more part-timer. If y'er interested, stop by anytime for a chat. Oh—and make sure yuh bring yer driver's license.

A MAN OF THE CLOTH

If you ever saw Sheila Sackowitz walking down the street, you probably wouldn't look twice. The girl was no Marilyn Monroe. We've been friends almost five years, so I'm just being objective.

Sheila and I would get together maybe once a month and have a regular girl's night out. One night, completely out of the blue, Sheila asked me if I ever answered any of those personal ads.

"Are you kidding?" I said. "Those ads are strictly for losers. Every guy is in his fifties and wants to meet twenty-year-old chicks. Forget it! I've got plenty of better things to do with my time."

"Julie, I just asked you a simple question. You don't have to get so defensive."

"OK already. By the way, since we're on the subject, what about you?"

"*Me?* I answered just one, and that was back when I was married."

"Sheila, am I missing something here? You answered a personal ad when you were married?"

"Yeah, it was right after Robert announced to me that he was gay. And that his lover would be coming up from Baltimore to spend the weekend with us."

"Unbelievable! You did say something about that a couple of years ago, but I thought maybe he was, you know, a little effeminate. But not technically gay."

"Believe it, Julie. Robert was a certifiable fag. And get this: He said to me that he wanted to share our bed with his lover, so could I sleep in the living room?"

"What did you *do*?"

"I bought a copy of *The New York Review of Books* and found an ad from a guy who actually lived in Baltimore."

"A straight guy from Baltimore?"

"You better believe it. He must of thought I was nuts. I asked him two or three times, 'Are you sure that you're straight?'"

"So, did you get together with him, Sheila?"

"I made a date with him for that coming weekend. In fact, I took the Metroliner to Baltimore."

"You're kidding!"

"No, Julie, I'm perfectly serious."

"Really? You went all the way to Baltimore on a blind date?"

"Look, there was no way I was going to be in our apartment with those two fags. I knew the marriage was over, so somehow this date made a lot of sense. In fact, that's why I picked this guy—because he actually lived in Baltimore. I guess part of the appeal was that it was somehow symmetrical."

"So, what happened when you got there?"

"I got off the train with all these commuters. It took a couple of minutes for the station to clear. Then there was just me standing there and there was this priest. So, I figured I was stood up."

"That's pretty shabby. The guy makes you come all the way to Baltimore, and then he doesn't show."

"I know. I felt like complete shit. I'm just standing there with my suitcase and the priest said to me, 'Are you Sheila?'"

"The guy was a *priest*?"

"That's what I thought! 'You're the guy who wrote the ad in *The New York Review of Books* and you're a *priest*?'"

"What did he say?"

"He said, 'No, I'm not a *priest*. I just *dressed* like a priest in case I didn't like you.'"

"Well, Sheila, at least he liked you."

"Yeah, well I was so disgusted, I was ready to get right back on the train. Also, he looked a lot older than he described himself in the ad.

"'I thought you said you were thirty-five,' I said."

"So, I lied a little."

"A *little*? Exactly how old are you?"

"Forty-five."

"Sheila, what did you *do*?"

"I was so mad at my husband, I decided I'd give this jerk a chance. So, I told him I was starving."

"Did he take you to a nice place to eat?"

"He took me to a supermarket."

"A supermarket?"

"That's right. He said he was on a tight budget. I mean, how much money do priests make? So, I picked out a couple of steaks. And when we got up to the checkout, he sticks the steaks under his shirt and just walks out of the supermarket."

"What did you do?"

"I walked out after him. I guess the kid at the cash register must of been Catholic, so it didn't compute that a priest could steal."

"So, then what? You went up to his place?"

"That's right. Do you want to take a guess what kind of place he lived in?"

"I'll bet it was a hovel."

"A hovel? That's too kind. He had a furnished room with a hotplate on the floor. And his bed! The sheets were gray and had stains on them."

"So, what did you do?"

"Well, I figured, let me make the best of a terrible situation. I could always grab a hotel room if I had to. Anyway, I was famished, so I guess I was lucky that I like my steak rare."

"Did you eat on the floor?"

"Actually, he had one chair, which he gallantly offered to me. Then, when we were about half way finished eating, he yells, 'Let's *fuck!*'"

"You *didn't!*"

"How could I resist that approach?"

"What did you do?"

"Julie, if we had been in New York, I would have just walked out of there. But then I thought about those two fairies having sex in *my* bed.

"Well, I gritted my teeth, took off my clothes, and lay down on those disgusting sheets. And thought to myself—how bad can it possibly be?"

"So, you did it with the priest?"

"Yes."

"How was it?"

"Best lay I ever had."

OVEREATERS ANONYMOUS

"Hello everybody. My name is Tom and I am an overeater."

"Welcome Tom."

About half the group was noticeably overweight, while quite a few others were very thin. This is a good place to meet women.

Am I going to OA meetings under false pretenses? Not really. I am indeed a binge eater, one who is quite capable of packing on ten pounds over a lost weekend of nonstop eating. My story is a common one and everyone here has heard it many times.

"I am just a fat man trapped in a thin man's body." Several people nodded knowingly. We're all fatties here, no matter what we actually look like.

I decided to tell my bagel story. "I happen to like bagels. So, I go to Broadway Bagels every day and buy an "everything" bagel. Just one. If I don't limit myself, I could go through a dozen at a sitting." Almost everyone is smiling.

"So then, I think to myself, why not buy *two* everything bagels—one for today and one for tomorrow? That way, I'll save myself a trip."

Everyone knows what's coming next: how I ate both bagels as soon as I got home and went to store the next day and bought four… and then eight the day after that…

When I finished, almost everyone was laughing. I mean, all of us could do the math.

After I sat down, I looked around and saw several attractive women in the audience. The tall, very thin women are anorexic. They may have once been overweight, but many have been painfully thin for years. One woman, in her mid-twenties, who was five-foot-nine and weighed one hundred fifteen pounds, had told me that she goes into a panic if she gets even an ounce over that weight. I've heard variants of that story many times.

A very good looking guy, maybe in his late twenties stood up to speak. "My name is Barry and I am an overeater."

"Welcome Barry."

"I am not only an overeater. I am an alcoholic, a drug abuser, a compulsive gambler, a hoarder and a clutterer. My only saving grace is that perhaps because I am also a workaholic, I have been able to hold on to my job.

"I've managed to put away a large pizza, a Junior's cheesecake, and two six-packs in one evening. I've been evicted because my apartment was a fire hazard and I've gone bankrupt twice. So, when I hear all *your* stories I ask myself, 'Who am *I* to judge?'"

Barry continued to talk about how hard it has been to deal with multiple addictions, and how he has come to accept that only complete abstinence can work for him. And that this realization made him so much more accepting of the challenges that the rest of us face.

When he finished, he got a heartfelt ovation. He bowed his head modestly and sat down. Even *I* was touched by his frankness and wondered if I could ever let it all hang out the way he had.

Next up was an angelic young woman who immediately grabbed everyone's attention. "My name is Mary and I am an overeater and a sexaholic."

"Welcome Mary."

"You know eating and sex are very similar activities. They're both physical. They're both social. They involve the senses, and they can be engaged in alone, with another person, or even with whole groups of people.

"I am so compulsive that I've had sex on subway stations, in movie theaters, in restaurants, and even during a church service … but not in *this* church." Most of us laughed.

This amazingly innocent looking young woman went on to tell one lurid tale after another, some involving celebrities, politicians, and a couple of religious leaders. When she finished there was stunned silence.

And then, one after another, we stood and began clapping. I saw tears flowing down her cheeks. It must have been tremendously difficult for her to have revealed so much of herself. Finally, she sat down. After the applause ended, there was complete silence.

Even though I had to be at least twice her age, I couldn't keep fantasizing about how nice it would be to make love to her. What's that tag line for the New York State Lottery ad? Oh yeah, "You never know." Dream on, Tom.

I can't recall how long it took until the next person spoke, but I do remember the end of the meeting. After the closing prayer, Barry, the young man with the multiple addictions made a beeline for Mary. She smiled at him and they began to chat. It was nice to see them together.

I left the church and walked across the street to my car. It was a beautiful summer evening, and was just getting dark. I watched the traffic lights along First Avenue, one after another changing from red to green. Then I looked back across the street at the church and saw Mary coming out. I was surprised that she was alone. When the light changed, she crossed First Ave., saw me and waved.

I told her how touched I was by what she said and she thanked me.

"I'm headed uptown if you'd like a ride."

"That would be nice."

"You know, I'm sort of puzzled about something. Would it be OK if I asked you a question?"

"Sure."

"Well, as soon as the meeting ended, I saw that guy with all the addictions rushing over to talk to you"

"Yes, Barry."

"Do you *know* him?"

"No, I don't think I've ever seen him before."

"Well I'm sort of curious. He seemed really anxious to meet you."

"Yes, I noticed that."

"And I saw the two of you talking. So, I was kind of surprised that he didn't at least walk out with you."

"Yes, that *was* a little strange. One minute he was really friendly, and then, very abruptly he said he had to go and rushed off. I think I must have said something to upset him."

"*Really?*"

"Yes! He had asked me how long I had been a sexaholic. I told him I had been having sex since I was eleven. He seemed very sympathetic. I said that I would always be a sexaholic, but like any addiction, you need to deal with it every day of your life. Then he smiled and said, 'Yeah, *tell* me about it! 'And that was just before he suddenly walked away."

"Really? Can you remember what else you said?"

"I said that I have been abstinent for two years."

THE SEXIEST MAN IN THE CITY

1

I am an eighteen-year-old college student and I have slept with just one guy. Jason, my high school boyfriend, was OK I suppose. I mean, who could I compare him to? But I know that there has to be more—a *lot* more.

We made it for the first time on the night of the prom, and then a few more times over the summer. Weeks before he left for college, we had both kind of lost interest. Still, he'll always be my first, so I'm glad we parted as friends. But I keep asking myself—is *that* all there is?

The thought never crossed my mind to attend an out-of-town college. Since my freshman year in high school, I wanted to be a filmmaker. And that meant studying at NYU. My parents, who are loaded, were delighted that I would stay in the city. So, they bought me a nice two-bedroom condo just off Washington Square Park. Their only stipulation was that I have a roommate—a *female* roommate.

Some of the guys in my classes were nice, but maybe subconsciously I was looking for a somewhat older guy—someone who knew a lot more than *I* did. It was definitely time to take things to another level.

So, when my roommate, Tara, suggested that we go to a party she'd heard about, I thought, 'Why *not?*' We got there and saw a few dozen people blabbing away to one another—

93

business types, hipsters, and a sprinkling of what we called "the bridge and tunnel crowd" from New Jersey, Long Island, and the outer boroughs.

Then the door opened and in walked the most gorgeous man I had ever seen. Tall, with bushy prematurely graying hair, what appeared to be turquoise eyes, high cheekbones, a deep tan – well, you get the picture. He was wearing a powder blue summer suit and an unbuttoned white shirt—and I could just make out what appeared to be a silver peace medallion. Silver and turquoise: I wondered if he could be part Indian.

I glanced around and saw that I wasn't the only one staring at him. Soon he was surrounded by four or five fawning women.

He was clearly enjoying this adulation, and I wondered if that might be *all* he wanted. Did he actually want to get laid, or was he addicted to the social foreplay? My friend Sara knew an extremely handsome priest who was always surrounded by worshipful women. But that was as far as he permitted things to proceed. Perhaps this party guy belonged to the church of latter day narcissists.

I enjoyed watching the women make complete fools of themselves. They were laughing at some probably inane remark he had made. But as I stared, I too could begin to feel the rapture.

I know I'm good looking, because guys are always hitting on me. But a couple of those women were really pretty, and they all looked hot to trot. If I joined them, why would he choose me—or any *one* of us, for that matter? Unless maybe he was planning a threesome, or perhaps an even larger grouping.

Then I had an idea. I laughed to myself, because it played to his narcissism. I took out my iPhone and very discretely began videoing.

Over time, one or two women would leave the group, and one or two others would join. This continued for more than an hour. I had far more footage than I would need. So I joined Tara to tell her about the role she would have in my plan.

"That guy over there? You want *me* to hand him a note?" She asked incredulously.

"Exactly."

"Why don't you give it to him yourself?"

"Because your doing this legitimizes the mission."

"Katlin, could you just lay it out for me in plain English? We're not living in a spy novel."

"Fair enough. Tara, you are a beautiful woman. *And*, a great actress." I paused to watch her preen. She was a year ahead of me at NYU and had already appeared in two or three off-off-Broadway plays and a breakfast cereal commercial.

I continued: "So a lovely young actress approaches a very attractive older man, and she tells him she has been asked to deliver this note. She leaves before he can reply."

"OK Katlin, *that* I follow."

"So, he reads the note written by the mysterious woman."

"And even if he thinks *I'm* gorgeous, he feels compelled to meet the woman who wrote the note.

But what did you write?"

"Here's the note."

Tara laughed as she read, "I'm a film student at NYU. I've just discreetly shot a video with my iPhone. You're the star. If you'd like a private screening, call me in a couple of days.

Katlin"

"Do you think he saw you videoing?"

"I doubt it. He and his concubines were far too occupied."

2

He called two days later. I played it cool, letting him do the talking. He *really* wanted to see the video. And *me!*

"I'll come to *your* place, say in about an hour?"

He gave me the address, and when I arrived, the doorman told me that I was expected. I could tell from his smirk that Apartment 16R was a popular destination.

When he opened the door, he looked very pleased. "I remember you," he said.

"And I certainly remember *you*!"

He invited me in and played it real cool, sitting opposite me.

"So, you're studying filmmaking at NYU?"

"Yeah, I just started last month. And you're my first leading man."

"I'm flattered."

"So, would you like to watch my video?"

"You *bet* I would!"

After I set up, he dimmed the lights and we sat back and watched the show. It was eight minutes long, and had been very carefully edited. Ryan was indeed the star. There he was with a shifting group of supporting actresses. It was a silent movie modeled on our solar system, perhaps the first ever set at a singles party.

At the end, he declared, "I *love* *i*t! You will be *great*! No, *no*! You *are* great!"

"*Thank* you!" I stood up, and then he stood. I went over to him and put my arms around him. He hugged me. Soon I felt his erection. I reached down and began to fondle him through his pants. He moaned. Then I felt his tongue in my ear.

I unzipped his fly. OMG was he *big*! I smiled to myself, knowing that he knew exactly what I was thinking.

With a practiced hand he unbuttoned my blouse, and then unhooked my bra. Did he know that he would be providing the on-the-job training opportunity of a lifetime? Was he aware that this was the first time I had actually tasted a man's cock? Or had my toes sucked? Or that this was the very first time that someone had actually licked every inch of my body?

We made love all night and I then left for school. On the walk to the subway, I thought that maybe I should ask him if we could record any future sessions for a sexual instructional video series: The Great Ryan, and his innocent young assistant, Katlin. Hell, *I'd* be the first on line to buy it!

Within a few weeks we had worked out a convenient arrangement: Every Tuesday we'd go out to dinner, and then stay up most of the night. Ryan never talked about what he did for work—or even if he *did* work. And neither of us ever said anything about what happened during the rest of the week.

I didn't care. I mean, what difference did it make? We both knew that what we shared was a schedule—not a relationship. I'm not saying that I was sexually addicted to him, or that I even *liked* him. But I *did* know that when we broke up, it would be very hard to find someone else who was such a skilled lover.

Sometimes we'd lie in bed just looking at each other. Once, I asked him what he was thinking. What he said really surprised me: that he was loving me with his eyes. And that he was making a video of me in his mind—one that he could watch when I wasn't with him.

I did love how he looked at me. Maybe part of it was how his eyes slightly changed color under different lighting. But most of the time, they were truly turquoise.

Later I thought about what he had said of always having an image of me in his mind. Was this his way of saying that our arrangement was just temporary? Or that he would never forget me? Or both?

My own motivations were much more transparent. Making the video was part of an elaborate plot to get Ryan into bed with me. And many years from now, he'll probably still be watching it. But as much as I loved having sex with him, if I had to choose between having made the video or being with Ryan, my choice would be a no-brainer.

It came down to love. I really *liked* sleeping with Ryan. But I *loved* the video. So did my classmates and our professor. He entered it in a school-wide contest—open to all undergraduate and graduate film students. When my video placed first, my parents were so overjoyed that they made a large contribution to the film school.

In a way, Ryan had made everyone happy and certainly me most of all. But then, one night as we lay in bed, he told me that he would be going on a business trip to China and would be gone for six weeks.

Was he *really* going to China? Or was this just *his* way letting me down gently? And then I thought: Does it really matter? By now he may have taught me everything that I could learn from him. Maybe it was time to move on. Still, I counted the days till he would return.

3

Had I missed *him* or just the sex? Soon after the six weeks passed, it became clear that he would never call. And surprisingly, it didn't matter. A few months later, I spotted him in the sports department of Macy's. When he caught me looking at him, he smiled, walked over, and asked, "Come here often?" He made chitchat, but said nothing about China, or even about not calling me. Still, some kind of apology, however insincere, *would* have been nice.

I imagined how I might have reacted if we were meeting for the first time. Surely, I would have felt the same impossibly strong attraction I had felt when I saw him arrive at the party. Perhaps he would always be the sexiest man I would ever meet.

All the while, he continued his patter. But then, he *really* surprised me. His tone changed from matter-of-fact to purely seductive. He told me how beautiful I was, and how he had never felt so attracted to anyone in his entire life. Then he whispered into my ear, "My dear, may I have your number?"

I was in *shock*! He misread my expression and persisted. "I *know*, I *know*! You must think I'm crazy! You don't want to give out your number to a complete stranger. OK, at least let me give you *my* card. I'm a podiatrist."

I stared at him, and then just shook my head "*No!*"

As I walked away, he called out, "Please *wait!* Just tell me why you won't give me your number. And why won't you even take my mine?"

I stopped and slowly turned around. "Fine. You already *have* my number."

He just stood there with his mouth open.

I continued. "Yeah, you already *have* my number. And… I have yours."

DREAMING OF JOLENE

1

Let me tell you just one thing about me: I have always been—and always *will* be—a strictly heterosexual male. End of story.

You're probably wondering why I find it necessary to make this statement. Well, back in the '80s and '90s, no one needed to say that. You were a guy, you were a girl, or maybe you were bi. That was *it*! You had three choices, not a whole fuckin' menu!

But today? *Shit!* I mean the definitions and sexual identities keep changing every couple of months. Which, I happen to think, is complete bullshit. I've always looked at it *this* way: You're either straight or you're not. End of argument. *Finito!*

Yeah, yeah, yeah—I know what you're thinking. Who is this ignorant, completely out of touch schmuck? Am I right? And you probably think I'm some old dude who can't stop blabbing about the good old days.

Whatever. I always thought fifty was old, so I've still got a couple of years to go.

Look, I'm sorry I got into all that shit, but if you're going to understand what happened to me, then you need to know exactly who I am and what turns me on. OK?

What I'm going to tell you all happened exactly ten years ago, almost to the day. It began on a Thursday night. I was living on the Upper Westside, and early one evening I saw this hot-looking chick in the supermarket. I could see that she was interested when we smiled at each other.

She was about as tall as I am, which is unusual for a girl. That's because I'm a shade over six feet.

I used to have a friend who wrote a book to help singles meet in the city. Her theory was that if a person was attracted to you, you could say *any*thing, and they would respond.

"Come here often?"

She laughed. "Is that the *best* you can do?"

"Look, I have this friend who wrote a book about meeting people."

"And did your friend suggest that line?"

"Well, you're talking to me, aren't you?"

We both laughed. Then I said, "I am *so* attracted to you!"

"Really?" she said.

"Well, yeah. Or else, why would I make such a complete fool out of myself?"

"You tell *me!*"

"So, can I have your phone number?"

"You know what?" she said. "Maybe it's better that we just have our fantasies."

"*You* are my fantasy!"

"*Exactly!* And I could never live up to that."

"Maybe our reality could be even better than our fantasy."

"*Our?*"

"Look, I'll bet you're as attracted to *me* as I am to *you.*"

"What makes you think so?"

"Because you're still talking to me."

"Point taken."

"I'll tell you what. I live just a few blocks from here. Come back to my place and I'll fix you dinner."

"Very smooth." We both laughed.

"Look," she said. "I'll tell *you* what: Here's my card. I've got some stuff to do now. Why don't you come over in a couple of hours?"

"*Great!*"

"OK, but remember what I said. Fantasy is better than reality."

"I'm going to prove you wrong."

2

I glanced at her card on my way home. Her name was Jolene and she was an art therapist, whatever the hell *that* meant.

The only time I ever heard of that name was in a movie I had seen years ago. The actress who played Jolene was maybe semi-attractive and pretty flat-chested.

But I loved the name. And *my* Jolene was the opposite of flat-chested. And she had very long, light brown hair. I supposed that in the '60s she would have been called a "hippie chick."

She had high cheekbones, big brown eyes, and a great smile. When *she* smiled, *you* smiled.

Jolene had long legs that looked like they never quit. You want a fantasy, Jolene? I'll tell you *mine*. I wanted those long legs wrapped around my head. But I'll bet she already *knew* that. And I'll bet she also knew a lot of other things.

3

Two hours later, I rang her downstairs bell and she buzzed me into the building. When she invited me in, she gave me a light kiss on the lips. I was smart enough not to push it.

We sat at her kitchen table drinking tea. We talked and talked and talked. And finally, we started to make out.

Slow and easy, I thought to myself. We had all the time in the world. But I had this huge erection and I knew that she could feel it. We must have been kissing for at least half an hour. Then she said, "Look, John, why don't we continue this tomorrow night?"

I just stared at her. I couldn't believe that she was going to send me home with the worst case of blue balls. Very, very reluctantly, I began to disengage.

She took my face in her hands. "We both have to go to work in the morning, and it's already past midnight. But tomorrow's another night."

Maybe she was right. And besides, horny as I was, I was in this for the long haul. Didn't mama say there'd be nights like this?

4

So, I limped the eight blocks back to my apartment and within a few minutes I was dreaming about Jolene. This time we went a lot further.

On my way to work, I laughed thinking about what Jolene had said about fantasy and reality. I could hardly wait to see whether or not she was right.

We had a date for eight p.m. I brought her flowers. She put them in a vase. Five minutes later we were rolling all over the floor, making out.

Soon I was humping her with my thigh. She arched her back and I could feel her shuddering. This was going to be easier than I thought. If I could do this to her with my leg, then just imagine how hard I would make her cum once I was inside her.

Our tongues were practically entwined. I thought she was actually going to deep throat me. I don't know where she learned to kiss like this, but she knew a hell of a lot more than *I* did! Teach me, Jolene, *teach* me!

I had never been so aroused in my life. Now we were lying side by side. She was stroking my cock through my pants and I was fondling her breasts through her bra. As much as I wanted to take things to the next level, I think I could have just kept doing what we were doing forever. This was, by far, the best sex of my life, and our clothes were still on.

I was smart enough to know that she needed to be in control, so I let her move things along at her own pace. Soon she unzipped my fly and reached in.

Now she had complete control. She had her tongue in my ear and my cock in her hand. She wasn't giving me any choices. In less than a minute she made me cum.

5

After we caught our breath, she kissed me and said, "There's something I need to tell you."

I just stared at her.

"I can't sleep with you right now."

I just starred. I didn't know if I was mad or sad, or maybe both.

"It's a physical thing. I'm not physically capable of having sex right now."

"Are you ill?"

"No, not exactly."

"Do you want to talk about it?"

"Maybe another time. Maybe if we get to know each other a little better."

"OK. Look Jolene, I want you to know something. You are the most exciting woman I have ever been with. I don't know what's wrong with you, but I really, really like you."

"I know that, John. I *know* that."

"Can I stay over? We can just hold each other. I'd really like to do that."

She kissed me. "Maybe soon, John. But not tonight."

I helped her up, and we kissed good night. By the time I got down to the street, I was thoroughly confused. What was *wrong* with her? Was she *dying*? Did she have a social disease?

As I walked, I considered a few more possibilities. And then I began to wonder what was happening to me. Look, I was thirty-eight years old, and maybe for the first time in my life I was actually falling for somebody.

Well, I could have done a lot worse for myself. And even if we found that we didn't have all that much in common, to paraphrase that old Captain and Tennille song, "Sex will keep us together."

103

I'm not a very patient guy, but I was willing to wait till Jolene was ready. I knew I could trust her. No matter what, I'd do whatever she wants. Isn't that what love really is?

I wanted to tell her that even though we barely knew each other, I would be there to help her with whatever she was going through. I mean, isn't that how you know who your friends are?

Even though we had only just met—and we had not yet been intimate—I felt I already knew her body better than any other guy she had ever been with. And even though we hadn't actually "*done it*" it still was, by far, the most exciting sex I had ever had.

I could stop looking. No other woman could come close. Ladies and gentlemen, I have an important announcement. My search is over: We have a winner!

When I got home there was one message on my phone. I was hoping that it was from Jolene, but it was from my friend, Larry.

He and I were basically party friends, not *real* friends. We partied together, occasionally talked on the phone, but never just got together.

It was too late to call him back, so I went straight to bed. Needless to say, I dreamed of Jolene.

6

When I woke up I decided to call Larry, and then Jolene. Maybe she would agree to see me tonight. We had not yet gone out on a real date. The only problem was what happened later. Maybe I could just walk her to her door and say good night. Fat chance!

So, I reached for the phone and called Larry. He probably wanted to tell me about some party. Well Larry, I hate to tell you, but my partying days are over.

When Larry picked up he got right to the point. "John, I heard you've been seeing someone."

"*Wow!* News travels fast! How did you even *hear* about us?"

"You know the old grapevine."

"So, you know her?"

"No John, not directly. But I know a couple of guys who *do* know her."

"Are we talking about the same girl? Her name's Jolene."

"Same girl." There was something in his voice I didn't like. He seemed to have taken on the tone of a funeral director. I was beginning to get the impression that just maybe it was *my* funeral.

"So Larry, what's the story?"

"In a word?"

"Whatever."

"John, you better sit down."

"Shoot!"

"Jolene's a *guy*!"

I didn't say anything. I *couldn't* say anything. My stomach was going through violent contractions. I was having a very bad case of the dry heaves.

Larry must have been able to hear me. He kept asking if I was OK.

It took me about half a minute until I could gasp, "No, not *really*!"

He then patiently explained everything. It turned out that Jolene was a pre-op guy waiting to have a sex change operation.

"You mean they haven't cut it all off yet?"

"You *got* it!"

"Holy fuckin' shit!"

"Yuh can say *that* again! So John, let me ask you a question."

"The answer is '*No*!'"

"No, you *didn't* fuck her?"

"Larry: stop and *think*! If I had fucked her, you don't think I would have noticed something?"

"Yeah, *that's* true. So John, why are you so upset?"

"You want to know *why* I'm upset? I'll *tell* you why I'm upset! I'm upset because never in my entire life did I ever meet someone so beautiful, so sexy, so sensual, such an unbelievable turn-on."

"Yeah, so what's the problem?"

"You wanna know the *problem*, Larry? *I'm* the problem! I just can't *do* it!"

"No?"

"*No!* I'm a *guy!* And Jolene, well *she's* a guy!"

"John, you just said you practically love her. And after she has the operation, she *will* be a woman. If you're so fuckin' attracted to her *now*, then just think how attracted you'll be once she's all healed."

"Larry, listen to my words: I'm a *guy!* And operation or no operation, *she's* a guy! End of story!"

STAY

1

Q: Why do men have holes in their penises?
A: So that oxygen can quickly reach their brains.

In other words, most guys *think* with their penises. *I* certainly do.

So, what do the ladies want? Was Cindy Lauper right, that "girls just wanna have fun?" Hey, that works for *me*.

2

When I arrive at a party, I usually just stand near the door and look around. Whom do I want to have sex with? And OK, who might want to have sex with *me*?

I happened to be leaving a party when I saw a truly gorgeous woman talking to a couple of guys. My coat was slung over my shoulder and I was headed to another party. But I *had* to talk to her.

I walked over, and without bothering to introduce myself, I reached out, lightly touched her cheek, and said, "Oh, what a *pretty* girl."

She looked at me with what appeared to be pure scorn.

"I must apologize," I said, ignoring the two guys. "I'm on my way to another party, or else I'd love to chat. So, here's my number. May I have yours?"

Through clenched teeth, she dictated her number. I thanked her, nodded to the two guys, and left the party.

A few days later, we went to dinner. I asked why she had given me her number, especially since I had been so obnoxious.

"*Obnoxious?* You were far *beyond* obnoxious."

"So how come we're sitting here together?"

"You mean, why would I go out with someone like you?"

"Yes."

"Well, on the day of the party, I had an appointment with my analyst. She told me that I should try being more friendly when I met people."

"So, I was kind of a test case?"

"I figured that if I could be nice to *you*, I could be nice to *any*body!" And she burst out laughing.

I learned across the table and kissed her. Then we rushed back to her apartment and jumped into the sack.

3

We made love again and again. In between, we'd tell each other stories. Hers were mainly about her family. She had grown up with an older brother and sister in Vineland, New Jersey, perhaps a whole world away from New York City.

When she was six or seven, she woke up one Saturday morning to find her brother sitting on her bed.

"Anna, I have a great surprise for you."

"*Really?* I *love* surprises!"

"I know you do. That's why I waited until you woke up. Are you ready for your surprise?"

"You *bet* I am!"

"Alright then, Anna. I want you to shut your eyes and keep them shut."

Then he asked her to get out of bed, to hold her arms straight out in front of her and start walking. He guided her as she carefully went step-by-step.

"OK, a little to your right."

They left her bedroom and moved down the hall.

"Do you know where we are?"

"Yes, we're right outside *your* room."

"Anna, are you *sure* your eyes are closed?"

"Of *course* they are! I don't want to spoil my surprise."

Her brother steered her into his room. And then he directed her to walk straight ahead. Her surprise was just a few feet away.

"How will I know when I've reached it?"

"I promise that you'll know immediately!"

And she did. Barefoot, she could feel something gooey and slimy. She screamed! Her brother ran out of the room laughing hysterically.

Anna looked down at her feet. She was standing in a pile of dog shit. She rushed to the bathroom and washed off her feet. Then she walked into her brother's bedroom, pulled one of his white shirts from the closet, and used it to scoop up the pile of shit, placing it under the blanket on his bed.

When she finished telling me her story, we were both roaring with laughter. Then we made love again.

4

What story could I tell Anna that would even come close to hers? I realized that the old tease would work.

"Well, there *was* something that happened to me a long time ago. But I don't want to bore you."

"Don't worry. I'm sure it's a great story."

"Well, it won't be nearly as good as yours. I mean, think of all the planning that went into your brother's 'big surprise.'"

"I know. It probably took him an hour to think that up."

"Well, let me start out by saying that your brother must have a much better imagination than I do. But, for what it's worth, here's *my* story.

"My friends and I were in the fifth grade. On our way home from school, we would pass the Avalon movie theater. There was a small frosted glass window about eight feet above the sidewalk on the side of the building. There was a stoop next to the window, and each day one of us would climb up and try to open the window. But it was always locked."

"Were you trying to catch someone taking a crap?"

"Of course! And preferably a woman."

"So *did* you?"

"No."

She looked at me expectantly. There had to be more.

I didn't say anything. She reached over and started tickling me.

I couldn't stop myself from laughing.

"I'm going to keep on until you tell me the rest of the story."

"Alright! Al*right* already!"

After she let up, I continued the story.

"The window was always locked."

She looked at me expectantly.

"Until one afternoon."

"Yes?"

"It was my turn. I climbed up on stoop, reached over, and started pushing up the window."

"Was anyone in there?"

"Yes!"

"A man or a woman?"

"A woman."

"What did she look like?"

"Well, I didn't get a very good look at her because I had to hop down and let each of my friends have a look."

"*Why?*"

"Because if they didn't see her, I had no proof that any of this had ever happened."

"So, *did* they see her?"

"Yeah."

"*Then* what happened?"

"She slammed down the window."

Then we were ready to make love again.

5

We stayed in bed for three or four days. Each time I said something about going home, she would look at me with a very serious expression and whisper, "Stay."

But eventually I *did* leave. I would be back the next evening.

When I returned, Anna threw her arms around me and then pushed me down onto her bed. It was as though I had never left.

But very soon, it became apparent that something *had* changed. The next morning, when I said I would go home soon, she didn't ask me to stay.

About a week later, I brought her to a party. She ended up sitting in a corner with some guy she met there. I got so mad I stormed out the door. She caught up with me in the street.

I glanced at her and kept walking.

"Why did you *leave?*"

"Why do you *think* I left?"

"Please, Steve. I really want to know."

"Don't insult my intelligence!"

"Steve, I'm *not!* I truly want to know what got you so mad."

"I didn't want to stay at the party like some schmuck, while you were with that guy. I'll bet you didn't even tell him you were with me."

"Look Steve. I didn't tell him because it was none of his business."

"Did you give him your phone number?"

"That's none of *your* business!"

"OK, Anna. See you around the quad." I had a sudden urge to go for a run. I ran all the way home, took my phone off the hook, and immediately fell asleep.

In my sleep, I heard a banging noise. I realized then that I was awake. I went to my door and opened it.

We just stood there staring at each other.

"Steve, do you still want me?"

I did.

6

The next morning, we worked out a kind of truce. If we went to another party, we would go our separate ways, but we would still leave together. *She* could be with whomever she wanted, and I could be too.

A few weeks later, as we walked into a party, I asked her to try not to be too obvious.

"What do you mean by *that?*"

"Anna, if you meet another guy, at least tell him that you can't leave with him."

"*Fine!*" she snapped.

"And if we're there awhile, and I'm not talking to another woman…."

Just then she grabbed my arm and pulled me over to a rather unattractive woman. Besides being quite overweight, she was rather homely.

"What's *your* name?"

"Amy," said the very surprised-looking woman.

"This is Steve. Good *luck!*"

And Anna walked off without another word.

I decided to make the best of things, although I had absolutely no interest in this poor woman.

"So what do you do, Amy?"

"I'm in my last year of medical school. And you?"

"Grad school."

"Let me guess. Math?"

"Kind of. Everything's mathematical now. Hey, is it OK if I ask you a question?"

"Shoot."

"Do you know much about kidneys?"

"Do you have a sharp pain?"

"No, more like an ache. But I'm not even sure it's my kidney."

"Is it here?"

I couldn't believe what she did. She had her hand on my crotch. I figured that either she wasn't in medical school—or she really *liked* me."

"Quick!" I said. "Give me your phone number!"

7

A few weeks later Anna and I were lying in bed with our arms around each other. I had been hoping that somehow things could be back to where they had been those first few days we had been together. Then Anna asked if I was sleeping with anyone else.

"In theory or in practice?"

"Yes."

"Ha! Ha! What about *you?*"

"I asked you first."

"OK, if I tell *you,* will you tell *me?*"

"Only if I *did* sleep with someone."

"Fair enough, Anna."

"Was it that nice woman I fixed you up with?"

"You mean the woman you picked out at random at that party?"

"Steve, I hate to tell you. She wasn't a random pick."

"You *planned* that?"

"I didn't say that either. What I *will* say is that I'm not dumb enough to introduce you to anyone who might make me jealous."

"Maybe you miscalculated."

"Maybe I did. Either way, I'm all ears." And she snuggled even closer.

8

Amy and I went out to dinner and then stopped at a liquor store so she could cash a small check. While she was there, she picked up a fifth of Clan MaGregor without asking me if that's what I drank. I wondered if maybe she'd taken me for an alcoholic who would drink pretty much any swill.

When we returned to her house, she immediately poured herself almost an entire water glass and began to take healthy gulps. As an after-thought, she asked if I would like some. When I declined, she happily went back to her drinking.

After putting away five or six ounces, she was ready for some action.

"Let's see if you're ready," she said, in an almost clinical manner. Let's see how that kidney is functioning."

Again, she placed a practiced hand on my crotch.

"Hmm. What have we here?"

Then she unzipped my fly, reached in, pulled out my cock, and began stroking it. Meanwhile, I reached over and began fondling her breasts.

"Are they as large as mine?" asked Anna.

"Larger. But remember, breasts are all fat tissue, and she has at least an 80-pound advantage in *that* department."

I continued my play-by-play description, ending with the summary supplied by Amy.

"Worst lay I ever had."

"*No!*" declared Anna.

"Scout's honor," I said, giving her the Boy Scout's salute.

"What a *pig!*"

"There's more."

"I can hardly wait, Steve."

"Then she picked up her glass and drank the rest of the Scotch. And poured herself another."

"*No!*"

"What can I tell you. That girl sure liked her Scotch."

"So *then* what happened? Did she start stroking your cock again? Like this?"

"*Yes!*" I gasped.

"And then?"

"We did it again."

"Really?"

"Yes."

"What happened after you finished? Did she *say* anything?"

"I don't remember."

"*Liar!*"

"Oh, yeah. She said, "'The first time was better.'"

9

"Now it's *your* turn, Anna."

"My turn for *what?*"

"Fair's fair."

"OK, all right!"

As jealous as I might get, I loved listening to Anna tell her tales. We had our arms would about each other, and no matter what she might tell me, I would not let go.

"Remember that guy I was talking to? At that party where you met Amy?"

"Sure. The one with the scraggly beard and the pot belly."

"Well, I'll bet Amy has a few pounds on *him*."

"OK, I know who you're talking about."

"So, we went out to eat. Now you know, I'm not a fast eater."

"Don't tell me he gulped down his food and started taking food off *your* plate?"

"He did it without even *asking*! I was still working on my steak when he started cutting off pieces and wolfing them down!

"I was getting so disgusted, I began to change my mind about going to bed with him."

"*Did* you?"

"Well, when we got back to my apartment, he was *still* hungry. He went into the kitchen and started opening the cupboard doors. He took out a can of creamed corn, opened it, and began spooning it down."

"Didn't he want to warm it up?"

"No. He couldn't wait."

"So, did he have that kind of appetite in bed?"

"Well, not exactly. I started stroking him through his pants."

"Yeah?"

"Thirty seconds!"

"*No!*"

"I think that may be the all-time record."

"Boy, you've got yourself a real winner!"

"Yeah. Maybe your girlfriend Amy can whip him into shape."

10

I am hardly a relationship expert, but it seems as though couples that want the same things will stay together, while others drift apart. Anna and I loved our time together. But we also loved having sex with other people. We could joke about it after each encounter, but we both knew that our promiscuity was driving us apart.

We would fight and then make up. We tried having an open relationship. We tried going to swings. In desperation, we even tried monogamy.

One evening, at a party where we were each doing our own thing, Anna overhead someone talking about us. Later, as we lay in bed, she told me what he had said. She imitated his deep voice.

"You want to know what's wrong with the two of them? They are both sluts!"

This made us laugh. But we agreed that he really had us pegged. When the Captain and Tennille sang, "Love will keep us together," they weren't singing about a couple of sluts.

Finally, we agreed to an amicable split. We would try to remain friends. And amazingly, this arrangement worked for a while. But over time, we drifted further and further apart.

Unlike Edith Piaf, I *do* have regrets. Those first few days with Anna were, by far, the happiest of my life. We were alone in the world. Other people existed only in the stories we told each other.

What I would give to have those few days back again. No one could ever make me as happy as *she* did. Life is about choices. Once made, they never can be taken back. We don't get do-overs.

Still, even now, I wonder what might have been if only I had stayed.

Part III

NOODLEMAN'S NEW YORK

Stanley Noodleman and his friends lived in a parallel universe. Guys in their late thirties, they still lived at home, had crappy jobs, and managed to go through the sexual revolution without ever getting laid. And yet, they all had dreams.

NAKED IN THE WORLD

Let me introduce myself. My name is Stanley Noodleman, I work part-time at the post office, and I still live at home. Somehow I always manage to run out of money halfway through the next pay period, so it's a godsend that I live rent-free. My mother keeps reminding me, "Stanley, you can't lead a full-time life on a part-time salary."

Last year, when my father was dying, I heard him asking my mother, "What's going to happen to Stanley when I'm gone?"

"Don't worry, Max. Stanley will be just fine. He just needs some time to decide what he wants to do with his life. He's only thirty-seven."

What else can I tell you about me? That I'm a little overweight? OK, I'll level with you. The last time I went for a check-up, the doctor told me I needed to lose at least a hundred pounds.

And one other thing: I really like women! The only problem is that a lot of them don't seem to like me. I've dated a lot of women, but none of these relationships worked out. Actually, I've never had a second date. Go figure.

There's something that I do every Saturday night since my father passed away. That's when my mother is out playing mahjong with the girls, and I have the apartment all to myself. I hate to admit it, but Saturday night is the high point of my week.

Right after my mother leaves, I run the water in the bathtub and take off all my clothes. Then I open the front door and adjust the lock so that when the door shuts, it locks automatically. There are seven other apartments on our floor. If you look closely, you'll see a mark on the hallway floor exactly 12 feet from my door. That's my all-time record.

So this is what I'd do. I open the door real wide, count to three, sprint to the 12 -foot mark, stop on a dime, spin around, and come flying back, just as the door is about to slam shut. And let me tell you, leaving the automatic lock on makes this extremely exciting. Like playing Russian roulette with real bullets.

This is a ritual I carry out every Saturday night. Did I ever lock myself out? Funny you should ask.

One night I decided to try for a new all-time record. Would you believe I was going for 12 feet, 6 inches? Remember, if I don't make it back in time, I'll be locked out. And I'm naked.

O.K. – here's to nothing! I open the door, run out to the 12 foot 6 inches mark, spin around, and rush back. Just as I reach out for the door, it slams shut.

SHIT! I push on the door. It's locked! I look under the doormat. No key. That's IT! I'm finished! Somebody'll open their door and see me. Or I'll be stuck out there till my mother comes home. How will I explain THIS one to her?

Maybe I can try to break down the door. No, too much noise. And besides, it's made of steel. Get the super's key? But then HE'LL see me—and probably tell my mother.

I know—I'll go up to the roof! That's IT! No one'll see me up there. It's dark.

So, I rushed up to the roof. Two steps at a time. Three flights. When I got the roof door open, I was gasping for breath. Don't die NOW! I don't want them to find me this way.

OK, I'm safe up here, but it's cold. I can't stay here. I gotta get into my apartment. But how? I know! I'll climb down the fire escape. But I'm afraid of heights. Don't...look. . .down. Don't.. look. ..down. OK, I'll do it. And besides, what other choice do I have? The thing is, I gotta go down the fire escape that's in the front of the building. If anybody looks up from the street, they'll see me. They'll see this big fat naked man climbing down the fire escape.

I have to do it. So, I edge over to the ladder and start climbing down. OK, don't look down. Don't look down. So far, so good. Three steps. Easy does it. One step at a time. I'm shaking like a leaf.

The ladder is vibrating. Don't look down. Five steps. I'm getting there. OK—nobody saw me. Keep going. One step at a time. I'm almost there. Sixth floor. There's the Edelstein window and the Fefferberg window. Their lights are out. Good sign.

One down, two to go. It's getting easier now. Closer to the ground. Not as far to fall. Shit! Don't look down! One step at a time. I'm getting there. Fifth floor. I'm passing the Rubino and the Schmuckler windows. Shit. The light's on. There's old man Schmuckler reading his paper. Since I was a kid, we called him "the schmuck!" Good! He's not looking out the window. OK, I'm passed him.

Two down, one to go. Easy does it. I'm not shaking so much anymore. I wonder if I would get killed if I fell from here. Shit! Don't look down. Just put one foot down at a time. Good. Only another couple of steps. That's IT! I'm there! Home free!

Except for one small detail: how do I get inside? What are my options? Wait for my mother to come home, knock on the window, and tell her I got locked out? No, she'd never buy it because she always keeps the fire escape window locked. In fact, triple locked. My mother's greatest fear is that one night a six-foot black man will creep through the window and rape her. I always wondered why a young black man would want to have sexual relations with my mother.

If I stay out here much longer, somebody'll see me. So what do I do? Break in? That's IT! I picked up this big potted plant that my mother had sitting out there and I smashed the window. In seconds, windows are opening all over the place. Upstairs. Downstairs. Across the street. Everywhere.

I managed to reach inside and unlock the wind. And then climb inside without cutting myself. NOW what? I'm safe inside. But how do I explain this broken window to my mother? It's the first thing she'll notice. She'll kill me! I gotta get outta here! Fast! She'll be back in an hour. If I'm not here, she can't yell at me. After she calms down, I can come back and face the music.

So, I put on some clothes and run out of the apartment. Where do I go? If I leave the building, someone'll see me. They'll know *I* did it.

I know: I'll take the elevator down to the basement. I just hope no one's in the elevator. Luck is with me, and I happen to have the key to the bicycle room, where I can hide until the coast is clear. Who goes bike riding at night?

I hide out for almost two hours, just to be on the safe side. I'm still trying tuh figure out what I can tell my mother. I think I'll just say I went out for a walk. That's believable, don't yuh think? What's she gonna do—ask me for witnesses?

That's my cover story—I went out for a walk. I just hope she buys it.

I take the elevator back up to the fourth floor and start to put my key in the lock, but the door is unlocked. There are voices coming from inside. Maybe somebody climbed in the window and was robbing us. That would actually be a big break for me because then my mother would blame THEM for the broken window.

But then I hear my mother's voice. "There he is now."

When I walked into the living room I saw my mother sitting in the wing chair and two big policemen taking up the whole couch.

Oh SHIT! I'm under arrest. Turned in by my own mother. I waited for them to go for their guns. I was ready to make a run for it.

"Officer Daley and Officer Esposito. This is my son, Stanley."

122

"Pleased to meet you,'" they both said, extending their meaty paws. I shook hands with them, trying to look each one in the eye.

"Same here."

Now I was really in for it. Arrested for breaking and entering my own apartment. Maybe I could get off with a suspended sentence as a first offender. Especially if my mother didn't press charges.

"Where WERE you? I came home from mahjong and the door was open. Then I saw that glass over by the window. Look over there, Stanley," she said, pointing at the mess I had made.

"My God! The whole window is smashed." I made a big show over walking over to the window and staring at it. I kept shaking my head. "What happened?"

"Where were you this evening, Mr. Noodleman?" Officer Daley asked.

"Actually, I went out for a walk. I think I left about 8:25. Or thereabouts." I was doing a pretty good imitation of Jack Webb on *Dragnet*.

"Stanley, I'm so glad you weren't home. Someone must have been lurking around on the fire escape and tried to break in," said my mother.

"Are you sure?" I asked. "I had some change on my dresser, not to mention my stamp collection."

"Go ahead and look," said Officer Daley.

I went into my room, opened a few drawers, and returned a couple of minutes later.

"Everything's still there. And it's all in order, just the way I left it."

"Stanley has a very neat room. Even when he was a little boy he kept his room neat. Isn't that right, Stanley?"

"Like I was saying before," said Officer Esposito, "the guy who pulled this job was definitely an amateur. No pro would have broken that window. That's a sure way to get spotted."

Now I started to get nervous all over again. "Did anyone actually see the burglar?"

"Are you KIDDING, Stanley? All the neighbors saw him. The police got a perfect description of him."

It's all over, I thought. They're playing cat and mouse with me. "Who WAS he?" I blurted out.

Officers Daley and Esposito looked at each other and didn't say anything. Then they looked at my mother.

"The neighbors saw this man without any clothes on. He was this 20-year-old *schwartze* (Yiddish for black person). They saw him climb through the window. It was a good thing neither of us was home because he had a big butcher knife. Your father—he should rest in peace—was always afraid that the neighborhood was starting to turn."

"Mr. Noodleman," said Officer Esposito. "We don't know if he was black. We've had a lot of conflicting descriptions. We got white, black, fat, thin, tall, short—you name it. But we'll keep an eye out for anyone in the neighborhood who looks suspicious."

The two policemen stood up. They shook hands with me and when they got to the door, Officer Daley told my mother to call them if she had any further leads.

When they left, my mother pointed to the couch. This meant she wanted to have a serious talk with me. And as I sat down I realized that my mother was no fool. She knew what had happened.

"Stanley, the policemen are gone now. So we can talk. Now I want you to remember—I'm your mother. I brought you into this world. I changed your diapers. You were this naked little baby. And now look at you! So, tell your mother the truth about what you did tonight."

"The truth?"

"There's nothing to be ashamed of. Remember, I brought you naked into the world, Stanley. Naked."

"I already told you, momma. I went out for a walk."

"You just went out for a WALK? And you wore your good sports jacket? The one I helped you pick out at Korvettes just before they went out of business?

"Alright, Stanley. I'm asking you for the last time what you did tonight."

"Come ON, ma!"

She didn't say anything. She just sat there. Then she took a deep breath and slowly let it out. "Stanley. I wasn't born yesterday. You think I don't know what you're doing when I'm out playing cards?"

"You KNOW?'

"Of course I know."

"You know what I'm doing every Saturday night?"

"You think I can't put two and two together? When I come home, the bathroom is still damp from when you took a bath. So, believe, me, I have a pretty good idea about what's going on with you every Saturday night. That's right, Mr. Big Shot!"

Then she looked right at me. My heart stopped. "So, tell me already, Stanley. How was your date?"

THE PERSONALS

1

Living with my mother was no bed of roses—except for the thorns. She never lets up about my getting married. "Stanley, I hate to remind you, but you're going to be forty years old."

"Yeah, ma, in two years I'm going tuh be forty years old."

"You'll be forty before you know it!"

"Not if you keep reminding me." She never gave up hope that I would someday meet the 'right girl.' I couldn't even meet the wrong girl!

"Stanley, I'm your mother." As if we had never been introduced. "Stanley, you can still marry a young Jewish girl and have babies. You can make me a grandmother.

"You want me tuh get married? OK, I'll get married. As soon as I meet someone I get along with. So, in the meanwhile, just let me have some peace." And I went into my room and shut the door before she could have the last word.

The more I thought about it, the more I realized that my mother was right. If I didn't find a girl soon, I'd never get married—let alone get laid.

It was time tuh take action. I decided to answer some personal ads. There was a whole bunch in *The New York Review of Books*, but I figured those broads would be too intellectual for me. So I decided tuh try *The East Village Other*. They didn't seem tuh mind what the ad said as long as they got paid.

"I'm tired of bland blondes who jump into bed," wrote one guy. Hey, send some of those bland blondes my way, I thought to myself.

Another ad said: "I'm 26, 6'1', 180 lb., well hung, like French culture, and love beautiful young chicks who want to ball. No fags, please!" Well, at least he's not tired of those bland blondes.

Most of the ads were from guys. Not too many girls were willing tuh take a chance. And I got the idea that a lot of the girls who did advertise were actually prostitutes. Who else would say they wanted to meet "generous guys," and wanted them tuh send a "tribute" or a "token" of their affection.

My friend, Irwin, had turned me on tuh the personals. He swore by them, although he admitted that, so far, he hadn't scored. Oh well, there's always a first time.

2

One day, Irwin and I were poring over the ads in *The East Village Other*. "Here's one, Irwin. Whadda yuh think? It says "Big buxom blonde into heavy B & D. What's B & D?"

Irwin didn't seem to have a clue.

"I dunno, Irwin. I think it's some kinda scotch. Anyway, the main thing is she doesn't say she doesn't like overweight men. So, I think I got a chance."

3

I called her that evening. "My place or yours?" she asked.

"I think your place might be better."

"Get right over here so I can whip you into shape." She sounded nice. A little strange, maybe, but very sweet. She had a pleasant voice. I took down the address and was on the subway ten minutes later.

She lived in a basement apartment somewhere out in Queens. It must of taken me two hours tuh get there. I went down the stairs and rang the bell.

Well, she was big. And she was buxom. And she was blond. She was also dressed entirely in black leather. She must

128

of been hot in those clothes. Instead of saying hello, she barked at me, "You're LATE! Get inside!" Then she slams the door shut and double locks it. I guess the neighborhood isn't too safe.

I go inside and sit down. 'Did I give you permission to *sit*?"

"Sorry. By the way, I forgot to introduce myself. Stanley Noodleman'" And I extended my hand. She just stood there and didn't say anything for, maybe halfa minute. Then she spit out these words: 'I know who the fuck you are, *asshole*!' I guess some girls like to talk dirty. Maybe it turns them on.

"Ex*cuse*   me?"

"Shut the fuck up!" she said. Then she picked up this whip. I was beginning to get the idea that she didn't like me. And that whip was making me nervous.

"Pull down your pants, you pathetic excuse for a man!"

"*What*?"

"NOW!"

So, what could I do? I pulled down my pants.

"Now kiss my boot."

"Whadda you kiddin? Is this some kind of joke?"

"YOU'RE the joke! Now kiss my boot!"

This was too much! I started to stand up. She hit me on the arm with her whip. Boy did that sting!

"Now KISS it!"

"I think I want to go home." I reached for my pants. Again she hit me with the whip.

"Whatsa matter fat boy? Don't tell me you're not into leather. Well, I'm going to help you acquire a taste. Now kiss my boot!"

So I kissed it.

"Now start licking it."

I knew I had to do something. "'LOOK, whatever your name is: If you don't stop, I'm calling the police.'"

"ASSHOLE! What the hell are you doing here? Why the FUCK did you answer my ad? Didn't you read what it said? B & D. Hey, if you're not into B & D, you're wasting my time."

"Lady, I don't even drink."

"What the fuck are you talking about? Look, just put on your pants and get the fuck outta here. You've got exactly ten seconds. One...two... three...."

I never got dressed so fast in my life.

4

The next day Irwin and I got together. When I gave him the blow-by-blow description of what happened to me on my blind date, he was very sympathetic. And then he said he had a confession to make.

"Irwin, don't tell me you ALSO answered an ad in *The Other*?"

"Actually, I put one IN *The Other*."

"What did it SAY?"

"It's a little embarrassing."

"TELL me, Irwin. I told YOU!"

"OK, but promise this stays just between us. I don't want to hear people talking about this on Kings Highway."

"Scouts' honor."

"All right, then. My ad said, 'I want to sail my big ship into your snug harbor.'"

"NO!" I blurted out. "You WROTE that?"

"Yeah. You know what they say, Stanley: 'truth in advertising.'"

"So, what happened? Did anybody answer your ad?"

"Yeah, three fags and one woman."

"Did you meet the woman?"

"Oh, I *met* her all right. She invited me over to her place in the East Village. She told me to ring her bell and she'd come downstairs to let me in."

"What did she look like?" I asked.

"Maybe so-so."

"Just so-so?"

"Well, I'd have to say, 'barely so-so. But look, I just wanted to get laid."

"So, she was fuckable?"

"Oh yeah, I'd say she was. Anyway, she says to come into the lobby, which turned out to be this hallway that stunk of urine. I was afraid that someone or some thing was gonna come outta a dark corner and grab me.

"And then she says tuh me, 'I was really turned on by your ad. You're a very creative person.'"

"'Thank you!' I said. 'Can we go upstairs?'"

"'In a minute,' she says. 'First I want you to show me something.'

"'Sure,' I said.

"And she said, 'I'd like to see exactly how big your ship is.'"

"Your ship, Irwin? You don't own no boat."

"Yeah, remember my ad, Stanley? 'I'd like to sail my big ship into your snug harbor'?"

"Oh yeah, right!"

"So, she wants me tuh take it out right there in the hall."

"DID you?"

"Whadda you CRAZY? In THAT hallway? What if somebody walked in and saw me with my cock out?"

"So, what happened?" I asked.

"Nothing."

"Nothing?"

"That's right, Stanley. Then she got really mad. She said that if l didn't wanna take it out right then and there, I was probably some kinda pervert, and she was afraid tuh let me into her apartment."

"This is crazy! She thinks you're a pervert because you *won't* take your cock out in the hallway?"

"That's right!"

"So what did you do?"

"I already *told* you, Stanley. Nothing happened. I just marched myself right outta there. And after the door closed behind me, she yelled, 'Yuh probably got a *small* one!'"

"So that was IT?' I asked.

"'Yeah, I got on the subway and came home. Then, just before I got to Kings Highway, I thought of a great thing I could of said to her. Remember when she asked me to show her how big my ship was? Well, I could of said to HER, 'How snug is your harbor?'"

SWINGERS

1

I'm gonna level with you, alright? We all wanna get laid. Am I right or wrong? What's that song about girls? They just wanna have fun? Well, for us it's "Boys just wanna get laid."

Now don't get me wrong. I'm not saying that's the only thing we want. But let's face it: it's right up there on our list. Don't worry: I'm not a sex maniac. But sex definitely does cross my mind.

OK, maybe I actually think about it a lot. I mean, if you're almost 40 years old and never been laid, trust me, you'd be thinking about it all the time.

So, one day, my friend Irwin says to me, "Stanley, do yuh wanna go tuh a swing?"

"What's a swing? A place with swings like a playground?"

"Don't tell me yuh never heard of a swing?"

"I'm telling yuh, Irwin, I never heard of a swing. So, what the hell is it?"

"Forget about the swings in the playground. You go to a party with a woman and the two of you split up. She goes looking for some guy tuh ball, and you look for a girl."

"Irwin, why go there with a girl if you're gonna split up?"

"Because it's for couples only. She's your ticket of admission. She gets you in there. If you showed up alone, they wouldn't let you in."

"Why not?"

"THINK about it! Stanley. If there was a swing around the comer and you could go there to get laid any time you wanted, would you go?"

"And I didn't have to go there with a girl?"

"That's right! How often would you go?"

"Oh, about three times a day."

"That's exactly my point, Stanley. The place would be filled up with horny guys like you and me, but not many girls."

Why not many girls?"

"Because girls don't need a place like that to get laid. A decent looking chick could go anywhere and pick up a guy who wanted to ball her. That's nature. Guys are always horny and girls could take it or leave it."

"So, Irwin, how do you find a girl who'll go with you to a swing?"

"That's the million-dollar question. I'm working on the answer right now. We need tuh find girls we don't give a shit about, who'll go there with us. Once we're inside, we can ditch 'em."

"Sounds great!"

2

A few days later Irwin and I got together with Alan, who was one of the guys we knew since kindergarten. Like us, he still lived at home.

Alan, an experienced swinger, was very happy to explain all the ins and outs of swinging.

"Yuh walk into this party with your date—actually, your swing partner. Everybody's got all their clothes on. It looks like a regular party. They always have good food. Everybody brings something. It's like a pot luck."

"I could go for that."

"I'm sure you could, Stanley. But remember, you're not there for the food. You're there for only one thing."

"Tuh get laid!"

"Right you are, Erwin! OK, so like I was saying, it looks like a regular party. People standing around talking, eating, drinking. If you walked in off the street, you'd never suspect what was gonna happen."

"How come they don't start screwing right away?" I ask.

"There's a very good reason why they don't start as soon as they walk in the door. You see, they have a rule. When the swinging starts, the door is locked. No one gets in. If you were naked and doing it to some chick, you wouldn't warn the outside door opening and closing. Let's say you were in an apartment house. The neighbors could see right in."

"That makes sense," said Irwin.

"You're damn straight it makes sense! And they got other rules. 'No' means 'no'. If yuh ask a chick tuh do it and she says 'no', then that's it! Yuh can't keep asking her.

"And then they got the rule that eating and fucking are in separate rooms. They got at least one room with beds or sometimes just mattresses on the floor. And they got another room where people are just hanging out, eating and drinking.

"So once the door is locked, what happens next?" I ask.

"That's when the fun starts. The first swing I was at, I was sitting next to this broad. While she was talking to another guy, she puts her hand right on my crotch."

"Holy SHIT!" Alan now had my undivided attention.

"So I reached over and started feeling her up, yuh know? First her tits and then I worked my way down. And meanwhile, I see other couples are going into the other room."

"The screwing room?" asks Irwin.

"Right! So, I kept fooling around with this broad, and then she asked me if I wanted to go into the other room. We went in there, and it was wall-to-wall balling. I never saw anything like it in my entire life. It was a regular orgy and I was right in the middle of it. I wished I had a camera."

"So do I!" I said. "So you did it with her?"

"I sure did! Boy, she was something else! We must have been at it for half an hour. I mean, she wore me out!

"And when we were finished—and this is the crazy part—I asked her for her phone number. And guess what she says to me?"

We both just sat there looking at Alan. How should WE know?

"She tells me, 'No.' 'No?' I said. We just DID it. You were fantastic! How can you say no? Yuh mean I wasn't any good?' I was beginning tuh get mad. And this whole time I'm still inside her." Can yuh fuckin BELIEVE it?"

Irwin and I just shook our heads. We couldn't believe it. This chick just DID it with Alan and she won't give him her phone number? She must be nuts or something.

Alan just sat there, with a look of amazement. "Then she tells me that she's been married for eleven years, and that almost every Saturday night they go to a swing. That keeps their marriage exciting, somehow. But she would never date anyone. Because that relationship could become something serious. And it could destroy their marriage."

"So, it's OK for her to screw a different guy every Saturday night as long as she never went out on a date with them?"

"Irwin, it's not as crazy as it sounds. I mean, if she does it right in front of her husband—and it turns out he was in the same room with us doing it with another chick—somehow that's alright. It's not cheating. The only thing is, I'm thinking, how can she do it with me, and then not want to do it again?"

3

Alan was definitely into something big. Imagine being able to walk into a room, pick out a chick, and do it with her.

He told us he could get us invited to a swing, but we had to bring dates, which brought us right back to square one.

Irwin kept after Alan to get his swing partner to ask her girlfriends, but he finally said to Irwin, "Look, just find your own dates. I mean, if yuh can't find swing partners, then you're probably still virgins."

Irwin and I talked a big game, but when you came right down to it, neither one of us had actually done it with a girl. And if yuh really want to know the truth, I never even got past first base.

But Irwin wouldn't give up. He told me that one way or another, he was going to go in a swing. Once he got in, he could meet all sorts of girls. And they would be our ticket of admission to a bunch of other swings. All he needed tuh do was get in the door. He needed a date.

But I was ready to throw in the towel. I had to admit that Irwin had more guts than I did. Maybe he was hornier or something, and I had to admire him. But I was pretty sure of one thing. By the time this swing thing blew over, Irwin and me would still be trying tuh bust our cherries.

Then one day, completely outa the blue, my mother asks me, "Did you hear what happened to Mrs. Schnipper." Mrs. Schnipper is Irwin's mother.

"No, ma. Was she in an accident?"

"*Accident*? What kind of accident?"

"So, what happened to her?"

"Irwin didn't tell you? Last night, he took his mother to a party."

"Irwin took his MOTHER to a party?" Holy SHIT! No! I can't believe it! I could feel my face getting beet red. My heart was racing.

"Stanley, are you alright? Your face looks flushed, Should I get you a glass of water?"

"Sure, ma. But could you let the water run so it's cold?"

She came back, handed me the glass with one hand, and with the other, she checked my forehead.

"Stanley, I think you may be coming down with something."

"No, no, I'm alright. I may have a touch of indigestion. So what was this about a party?"

"It was the strangest thing. Mrs. Schnipper hasn't been to a party in over 30 years, she told me. But Irwin insisted that she come. So, they went somewhere in the city. Someplace on the

Upper Eastside, a tall building with a doorman in a uniform. And they brought a big pan of Mrs. Schnipper's cheese blintzes (sweet crepes)."

"I could go for some of those cheese blintzes right now. So, who was giving this party? Maybe they were relatives or something?"

"Stanley, let me finish, already! They walk in and it's all younger people. You know, people in their forties and fifties? Poor Mrs. Schnipper felt like she stuck out like a sore thumb. And Irwin didn't help things none. He didn't tell anybody that she was his mother. He introduced her by her first name. Can you believe that?"

"Holy SH.. er, no! No, I can't. Since I was a little kid, she was Mrs. Schnipper. I didn't even know she HAD a first name."

"So where *was* I? Oh yes! She sits down and then Irwin just disappears. She tries talking to the girl next to her, but the girl gives her the cold shoulder. Meanwhile, where's Irwin? And why did he bring her here? The people are so rude. In fact there were two couples actually kissing."

"Right there in front of Mrs. Schnipper?"

"That's not the worst of it. One of the man had his hand..."

"STOP! I don't want to hear any more!"

"Stanley, what's wrong with you? Let me finish the story already. She's looking around for Irwin, but she doesn't see him. So she gets up to get have a nosh."

"What kind of food did they have?"

"She didn't say. Wait, maybe some chicken. A salad. Some rolls. A few plates of cookies. I think she said there were these little sandwiches. Maybe some coleslaw.

"So, she made herself a nice plate of food and sat down again."

"And she still didn't see Irwin?"

"Didn't I just get finished telling you he disappeared? She sees that some of the people are going into another room. So, she gets up and follows them. And what she saw, Stanley, you would not BELIEVE! People without their clothes on."

"WHAT?"

"Naked people! Naked men and women!"

"My GOD! So what did she DO?"

"She went from room to room until she found Irwin. He was having a nosh. I think, maybe a sandwich and some potato salad. And a pickle. So, she tells Irwin, 'I'm leaving this minute! Get me my coat!'"

"So, did he?"

"Of course! But when his mother was putting on her coat, the host told Irwin he had to leave too. He said something about breaking a rule. WHAT rule? Naked people have rules?"

"That is some crazy story!"

"You're telling ME? And it all happened last night. Irwin didn't call you?"

"No, this is the first I heard of it. Wow! Mrs. Schnipper must be pretty mad at him."

"Can you imagine what that boy did to his mother? Taking her to a party and just leaving her there by herself? And those terrible people taking their clothes off. What were they THINKING?"

"That was *terrible*! So Mrs. Schnipper must have been pretty pretty angry."

"Let me tell you: that friend of yours is in big trouble! Mrs. Schnipper grounded him for a whole month. He has to come home right after work—and no running around on weekends."

"Maybe I should give him a call to see how he's doing."

"Stanley, you do whatever you want. But you're such a good boy. I think that Irwin is beneath you. Look what he did. He broke his mother's heart.

"And let me ask you something: after THAT performance, what nice Jewish girl would want to marry him?"

Part IV

LOVE IN THE CITY

Do people fall in love in New York, get married, and live happily ever after? Is the City a song sung by Frank Sinatra about lovers sitting all night in Central Park, or a movie about meeting on the observation deck of the Empire State Building—or under the clock of the Biltmore Hotel? *Is* New York a City of love?

THE LAST OF THE GREAT LOVERS

1

Gene is possibly the smartest person I know and, in some ways, the dumbest. He can be unethical, and yet he'd do almost anything for someone he truly cares about. He is a perfectionist and is sometimes hypercritical. Gene is impulsive, calculating, but sometimes quite endearing. Most of all, he always has something going on, something that really excites him.

Gene and I became friends as teenagers. We went to parties together, tried to meet girls, and played ball in the park after school and on weekends. While I was on track to go to college and then graduate school, Gene was, at best a little better-than-average student.

Then, almost out of the blue, Gene's father threw him out of the house. He was a senior in high school, not yet seventeen.

Gene moved into the Sloan House YMCA on West 34th Street near Ninth Ave. He found a low-paying office job, managed to get his high school equivalency diploma, and then joined the Army.

You would think that he would have been unhappy and resentful, but Gene confided that his father had actually done him a great favor. Now the Army would pay for his college education, provide him with valuable training, and at the same time he'd get his military obligation out the way. Back in late 1950s, we still had the draft, so most guys would eventually have had to deal with it one way or another.

Six years later, Gene was back in Brooklyn with little to show for his time in the Service. He had about two years' college credit, and had learned some German. He enrolled in Brooklyn College as a twenty-four-year-old junior, using the G.I. Bill of Rights to pay his living expenses. In those days, the four-year public colleges in New York were still free.

Now he knew what he wanted to do with his life. He became a philosophy major, specializing in the existentialists. The college had an excellent philosophy department, and Gene's dedication, enthusiasm, and scholarship were greatly appreciated. He was truly home at last!

Early one morning during his senior year, Gene did something that his professors would talk about for years. He had been writing his honors thesis on Kierkegaard, his favorite philosopher. But, perfectionist that he was, Gene begged for extension after extension. Finally, his advisor laid down the law. The paper must be delivered to the department office by Friday morning at eight a.m.

Gene knew that, in the words of another idol, Jean-Paul Sartre, "the game was up." He worked virtually non-stop for the next seventy-two hours, fueled by an entire bottle of "NoDoz." He laughingly recalled the Army training films he had watched about the torture American soldiers would endure if captured by the enemy. That, by comparison to what he was now putting himself through, would be a walk in the park.

On the third night, he caught himself nodding off. He had mental images of himself acting in an old black and white Army training movie. He was an American prisoner of war being yelled at by the "Aggressors" who were wearing helmets, each topped with a long strip of wood, making it look like a helmet with a Mohawk haircut. His laughter stopped him from falling into a deeper sleep.

On Friday at 7:40 a.m. Gene finished typing. There was no time to proof the paper one last time. He walked over to the college, and made his way to the Philosophy Department office. The lights were on, and when he opened the door, he saw several professors standing around. They stared at him. He was unshaven, disheveled, and there were dark semicircles under his eyes. And he was visibly shaking.

The department secretary asked, "Gene, how can I help you?" He didn't answer. The professors standing nearby began to grow concerned. But luckily, Gene then snapped out of it. In a very matter of fact voice he answered, "Yes. When Professor Kierkegaard gets in, could you please give him this paper?"

2

Despite Gene's devotion to his studies, he always checked out his classes for pretty women. To his surprise, one of them approached *him* after a sociology class. She said that she really appreciated his seriousness and his intelligence.

Gene could not believe his luck. Marlene was an education major and would begin teaching third and fourth graders in the fall. They began making out on the third date, and took it from there. Then he completely caught her off guard by proposing.

She didn't answer at first. But when she did, it was *his* turn to be caught off guard.

"I don't see a ring."

"OK, Marlene. You will see a ring next week."

Exactly one week later he kneeled down on one knee and asked, "Marlene, will you marry me?"

Marlene took a deep breath. "Yes, Gene, I will!"

He handed her a tiny box.

Marlene opened it, and put the ring on her finger, while Gene got up and then sat next to her. She was smiling as she admired the ring. This went on for a couple of minutes. It was one of the happiest moments of her life, and she let it stretch out.

Then she threw her arms around Gene and kissed him. She had picked herself a real winner! In just a short span of time she will have earned *two* degrees—a BA and an MRS!

3

In the middle of his last semester Gene received the greatest news of his life: Cornell offered him a full scholarship.

If things went according to plan, he would earn his PhD in four or five years. He would then be set for life.

Marlene was the first person he called. He was so excited that he didn't pick up on her lack of enthusiasm. But they would celebrate that night.

When he got to her house that evening, Marlene looked very sad. "Gene, we need to talk."

What was going on? Was she *mad* at him?

"Gene, this is very hard for me to say. I still love you, but this engagement isn't working out. We want different things in life."

"I thought we wanted a life together."

"So, did I! But you'll be going to Cornell, and I'll be working for the Board of Education. I already know which school I'll be assigned to."

"You could get a job in Ithaca!"

"I don't *want* be in Ithaca! I want to stay in New York. This is where I grew up. This is where my friends are."

He realized that there was nothing he could say that would change her mind. He stood, looked at her one last time, and then walked out of her house. When he had gone a few blocks, he began to realize that it was probably for the best. If a woman could not help him realize his dream, then she was not the woman for *him*!

4

Gene called me when he got home. He had called earlier about Cornell, and now this.

"So how do you feel, Gene?"

"Actually, pretty good."

"No regrets?"

"Well, Steve, maybe this was the best thing that could have happened to me—*besides* the scholarship."

"I don't know. Let me ask you a question. How did you feel when she gave you back the ring?"

"She didn't give it back."

146

"*Really? Shit!* That ring must have set you back quite a few bucks. What was it, three-quarters of a karat?"

"It was almost a karat."

"So you're not mad?"

"Not at all. Especially since I paid just fifty bucks for it."

"That's *impossible!*"

"Well, I'm not going to go into details, but if you took that ring to several jewelry stores, you wouldn't get more than sixty or seventy dollars. So I got a big bargain."

"You certainly did! And I'd love to see Marlene's face when *she* goes to get it appraised."

5

In late August, Gene left for Ithaca, determined to keep his nose to the grindstone. And *did* he! He got all A's, his professors loved him, and he already had the rest of his life carefully mapped out. He would earn his PhD, and find a teaching position at another Ivy League school. He would publish, become an academic star, and along the way, marry the most fantastic woman.

When Gene returned in June, he rented a furnished room in Brooklyn Heights, not far from where I was living. We hung out a little, but he was very busy preparing for the fall semester. Then something happened: Irene.

No superlative could do justice to this woman. Although a natural born sceptic, even *I* was convinced that just maybe, she was "the One."

I didn't get to meet her until a few weeks later at their engagement party. When Gene gave me the news and invited me to the party, I asked what the rush. He babbled something about striking while the iron was hot. Then he showed his practical side. Look, if I didn't propose, some other guy would grab her. This way, even though I'll be more than two hundred miles away, I can still keep her out of circulation.

What *is* she, I thought to myself—a library book?

When I got to the party and met Irene I was completely underwhelmed. She was mildly attractive—I'd give her maybe a seven—but the real problem was that she was a secretary, and to put it bluntly, no Einstein.

The party was in Irene's family's apartment. Her parents were very friendly, and obviously extremely proud of their daughter. And I thought: She's marrying a really smart guy who may someday be a prominent philosopher. But what about *her*? Not only was she doing almost nothing with her life, she didn't exactly appear to be Ivy League faculty wife material.

Irene's mother consoled me, "Don't worry, Steve. I'm sure you're next."

Then her father added, "Don't worry, Steve. There's no rush." He winked at me as his wife gave his arm a playful push.

Irene kept reminding everyone that she was engaged to a Cornell PhD candidate. Not a very accurate statement, since you don't attain that lofty status until you have at least another couple of years under your belt. But why tell her this and spoil the fun?

Gene took me into the kitchen. "Isn't she *great*?"

"Do you want my frank analysis?"

"You don't like her?"

"Gene, she seems very sweet. But all she talks about is being engaged to a Cornell PhD candidate."

"Yeah, it *is* pretty embarrassing."

"Look, if you really love her, then none of that matters."

Just then, Irene rushed in and dragged Gene into the living room to help her open their presents. I remember how she pretended to be modelling a negligee as everyone ooooooooohhed and ahhhhhhhhed. Gene whispered to me, "Am I obligated to get an erection?"

I knew then that this might be just a summer engagement. But still, it was *his* choice.

A couple of days later, Gene called.

"Still engaged?"

"Of course, you idiot! Look, I want to fix you up with someone."

"Forget it! I *hate* blind dates."

"*Trust* me! Wendy is beautiful! A perfect ten!"

"Really? How do you know her?"

"She's Irene's closest friend."

"So I must have seen her at the party."

"She couldn't be there. Her mother was in the hospital. But she's better now."

"Look, thanks for thinking of me, but I just don't do blind dates."

"Steve, I promise that you will really, really like her. She's beautiful. She's very intelligent. She's funny."

"Gene, maybe you should be engaged to *her*."

"I think that's not an existential possibility."

"*Ha!*"

"Just call her. If she sounds nice, then make a date. If not, then no harm done."

"OK, why *not*?"

6

The next evening, I called Wendy. Minutes into our conversation I was smitten. She was my soul mate! And, who knows: maybe I was hers. Two hours later, we finally hung up. I would meet her after work the next evening. We would take the subway back to Brooklyn, and go to a restaurant near her house.

The minute we hung up, my phone rang. Before I could pick it up, I panicked. What if she were calling back to cancel?

"Hello?"

"Steve, I've been trying to reach you for hours! You must have been talking to Wendy! So, how do you like her?"

"Gene, calm down. Take a deep breath."

"How long were you talking to her?"

"About two hours."

"What did you talk about?"

"You know, this and that."

"Be more specific."

"Take it easy, Gene. She sounded great. We're going out tomorrow evening."

"What are you doing? Where are you going?"

149

"Look Gene, it's late. I'll tell you what. I'll answer all your questions after I see her."

"OK, call me as soon as you can."

7

I knew Gene sometimes wandered pretty close to the edge, but this was really strange. Here he's engaged to one woman, but possibly obsessing over her friend. Unless maybe he was just so happy that he wanted *me* to be happy too. Yeah, right!

The next evening, Wendy met me in front of her building at 5 pm. She was tall, had long blonde hair, and was fairly pretty. As we walked toward the subway, she took my arm, which made me feel very proud. We didn't say much until we got downstairs to the platform.

"Steve, can I ask you for a really big favor?"

Sure, I thought. *Any*thing!

"Do you think we can take the local instead of the express?"

"Wendy, I want to tell you something. I am really happy to be with you. You could have asked me for a much bigger favor."

She squeezed my arm slightly, which made me feel still better. She was just so nice to be with. I began to understand Gene's seeming obsession.

Then she explained. "I have a tremendous fear of bridges. So I always take the local through the tunnel, even though it takes ten minutes longer."

"You know, I used take the local too, but that was because I got a seat."

She laughed, and I almost tried to kiss her. Then the train came and we got to sit together. We chatted until the train entered the tunnel. She began to shake. I put my arm around her. Soon she was shaking even harder. I thought some people were looking at us.

"Are you OK?"

"No-o-o, not real-l-l-y."

"OK, don't worry. I'm just going to hold you, and you're going to be fine. I promise, I won't let anything happen to you."

I was getting very confused. It was really nice to hold her, but her behavior was becoming increasingly strange.

When we finally got out of the tunnel, she began to relax.

"Wendy, you told me you were afraid of bridges, but it looks as though you're *really* afraid of tunnels."

"Bridges are *much* worse!"

I didn't know what to say. Were these just phobias, or was she nuts?

Me? I'm really afraid of heights. I can't climb a step ladder without shaking. So I *do* have a degree of empathy. But this bridge and tunnel thing? Maybe it was just the tip of the iceberg.

We continued riding till we reached her stop, and as we walked to the restaurant, she was almost back to her old self. But something had changed. And then she said, "Steve, you know, I really don't feel like eating. Do you think we can just call it an evening?"

I didn't know what to say. So I just played it safe. "OK, would you like me to walk you home?"

"No, that's alright. I'm just a few blocks from here."

She leaned over, kissed me on the cheek, and then walked off.

As I watched her walk away, I still felt very conflicted. Should I rush after her? As she rounded the corner, I turned and headed off the other way.

When I got home, my phone was ringing. It had to be Gene.

"So how did it go with Wendy? Tell me *every*thing!"

8

Gene broke off his engagement to Irene a week later. I felt kind of sorry for her. She had probably lost her one big chance. The next day he called Wendy. When he asked her out, she hung up on him.

151

A few days before going back to school, he bought a used Chevy Impala convertible, which he loved. Everything was still going very well for him. He called me when he got home for winter break to tell me that he had met another woman and was in love.

Gene had placed some signs around school offering rides to students who would share expenses. Doreen was one of the students who responded. She looked like Elizabeth Taylor.

But a day later, he went out on a blind date that had been arranged before he left Ithaca. Since he wanted to pick up a book from me, he brought his date with him. They stayed for a little while, and then went off to dinner. Susanne was quite attractive. I liked the way she smiled at me, but maybe she was just being friendly.

The next day Gene called to ask me what I thought of Susanne. I said she's as good as it gets. He said that he agreed with me. In fact, he liked her so much, that he was going to dump "Elizabeth Taylor."

Things did not work out quite as planned. When he called Susanne to ask her out again, she thanked him, but said she just wasn't that into him. I thought of asking him for her number, but sometimes it's best to just let things lie.

In late March, Gene called me from Ithaca. He had some great news! He had indeed taken my relationship advice to heart, and had vowed not to make the same mistake again.

"So, Gene, if I understand you correctly, you're calling to tell me about a woman."

"*Bingo!*"

"But this time you're not rushing into another engagement."

"Steve, you're a mind-reader!"

"Hey, it doesn't take a mind-reader to figure out *your* problem."

"When you're right, you're *right!* So I can promise you— not another engagement. Remember the woman I gave a ride to during winter break?"

"Sure. Elizabeth Taylor, aka Doreen."

"Well, congratulations are in order! We got married last week!"

9

A couple of months later, Gene slipped in the bathtub, badly injuring his back. He ended up in New York Hospital, which is affiliated with Cornell. When I went to see him, he was in traction. Doreen, who was in her last semester, had stayed behind.

It would be several months until Gene could return to school. When he was finally able to make the trip, I went along with him to help with the driving. I would be staying with them for just a day or so. On the way, somewhere near Scranton, he casually mentioned that his wife was eight months pregnant.

When we arrived, Doreen was overjoyed to see him, but he seemed distracted. It turned out what was bothering him was that the workmen were still there, putting the finishing touches on a new kitchen floor.

The next morning at breakfast, Gene asked Doreen to reheat his coffee for another six seconds. Then he held up a piece of toast, which was slightly burned in one corner. After that, he asked her to re-reheat the coffee for another four seconds.

"For Christ's *sake*, Gene!" I yelled. "You ate Army chow for six *years*! How many times did you send *that* back to the chef?" I stood up, grabbed my bag, hugged Doreen, and was on the next bus to New York.

10

Gene junior was born just one month later. According to the announcement, he weighed in at six pounds, fourteen ounces. Good luck, kid! You're gonna need it!

Gene senior was making up two incompletes. His professors, who fully understood his circumstances, cut him a lot of slack. But I had a feeling that something bad was about to happen.

I'm not sure which came first, his difficulties with the department chairman or the breakup of his marriage, but five months after his return to Ithaca, Gene was back in Brooklyn. He stayed with me for a few weeks until he found a small apartment nearby. He never spoke again about Cornell, his study of philosophy, or even Doreen and Gene junior. Perhaps his only reference—and this came a few years later—was the scorn he felt for his ex-wife. She had remarried. "Would you believe that the guy's a *plumber?*"

Somehow, Gene got involved with real estate, and within only a few years, he was making tons of money converting rental buildings into condos. The whole trick, he explained, was financing each project almost entirely with borrowed money.

Gene rarely went to see his son, especially since he had a new father. Still, he voluntarily doubled his child support payments and set up a trust fund that would pay for his education all the way through graduate school. But he and Gene junior would remain virtual strangers.

11

We drifted apart soon after Gene sold his business and moved away from Brooklyn Heights. A few years later I heard that he had remarried—this time to a woman with a young daughter. They were living somewhere out on Long Island.

For a few years, we completely lost touch. Still, when the phone rang and I heard his voice, I was not at all surprised when he began talking about his marriage, which had recently ended. He said that while their relationship had been turbulent, he and Krista managed an amiable divorce. They still loved each other, but their differences were irreconcilable.

"You know, Steve, it's really a big shame. Krista was the only woman I truly loved."

I later heard that their irreconcilable differences were manifested by screaming arguments, a few police interventions, and one very suspicious three alarm fire.

I also learned that before he met her, Krista and her daughter were living on Public Assistance. "I'd like to think that I left them a lot better off than they were before I met them."

I realized that he said this without rancor or irony, and I felt a new respect for him. He had helped them out of love.

Again, he disappeared, leaving me to wonder if I would ever see him again. A year later, he called. He was in California, and was living with a woman named Theresa, who had just left her husband. They were in love.

Did I mention that Gene could sometimes be hyper-critical, especially with the women he became involved with? Theresa happened to be a personal trainer. Gene, who at the time weighed over 300 pounds, was constantly criticizing her appearance.

Well, she threw him out. That proved to be a major wake-up call. He knew he had to make a big change. He needed to lose weight and begin working out, so he could win her back. It took him more than a year, but he got into the best shape of his life. But by then, he had lost track of her.

He began noticing that women sometimes smiled at him. One day he saw Theresa in the supermarket. He waited until she spotted him.

"Gene, is that *you*? Is that *really* you?"

He waited a few seconds before just nodding.

"You look *amazing!* I never would have guessed in a million years that you could have done this."

Gene was gloating. He could see how badly she wanted him back. But he'd play it cool.

"How *are* you, Theresa?" he asked.

"Never better! My ex and I got back together."

12

Apparently, there wasn't enough room for the two of them in the entire state of California, so Gene decided to get a fresh start in south Florida. And it was there that he soon met a truly wonderful woman named Betty, who had come there from Jamaica a few years earlier with her husband and two children.

She and her husband had been childhood sweethearts, but after they arrived in Florida, he began to "fool around."

When she realized what was going on, she took the children and moved in with her sister. He came around and begged her to take him back. And then, maybe a few months later, he began staying out late one or two nights a week.

That's when she decided to leave him for good. He agreed to a divorce, and since then, he saw the children every Sunday. Then Gene moved in next door.

At first they just chatted, and then, there was a little flirting. Gene wondered about the ex-husband, but Betty assured him that there was no going back. The man was incorrigible.

Soon she and Gene were living together, along with Betty's two children. Gene loved Betty and both children. He told me that for the first time in his life, he was truly happy. Perhaps it didn't hurt that Betty was at least twenty years younger, and made Gene believe that he did indeed walk on water.

One Saturday afternoon, when Betty and the children were visiting relatives, Gene saw her ex-husband pull up in front of the house. A minute later he rang the bell. This was pretty strange, because the only time Gene saw him was on Sunday.

"Hi, Michael. Betty and the kids are visiting her sister."

"Gene, actually I came to see *you*."

"OK, let's go inside."

They sat down next to each other on the couch in the living room. For a minute, neither said a word. Then Michael began his story.

He told Gene how he and Betty had known each other since they were four or five, and how much he still loved her and their children. He knew he had fucked up, and that even if he and Betty got back together, he might still go back to his old ways.

Gene felt a grudging admiration for Michael's honesty, but he was puzzled. Why was Michael telling all this to *him*? He must *want* something. But *what*?

156

He decided to let Michael keep talking, hoping that he would explain what he wanted.

But then Michael began to grow agitated. Gene wasn't sure what to do. He was tempted to put his arm around the man to comfort him.

Finally, Michael said, "Gene, I want to show you something, but don't be afraid."

He pulled out a hand gun and held it pointed at the floor. He didn't do this in a threatening way. It was more like show and tell.

Gene waited and after several seconds, Michael put the gun back in his jacket.

Neither of them spoke for maybe a couple of minutes.

"Look, man, I even don't know what made me buy this gun. I'm so afraid I'm going to use it. If that woman don't take me back, I don't know *what* I'm going to do."

Gene didn't say anything. He knew there wasn't anything he *could* say. The two of them just sat there.

"Michael, I'm going to tell you something that I never really told anyone before. Maybe because it's too painful—or because I could never admit it to myself.

"I have a son—a son I've rarely seen since he was a baby. I walked out on him and his mother a very long time ago. Yeah, I sent child support every month, but I wasn't there to see my son grow up. My wife remarried, and her husband is my son's *real* father."

The two of them sat there in silence for several minutes.

Then Michael stood. And Gene stood. They stared at each other for a while, and then they hugged.

As Michael left the house, Gene called after him. "We will do our best to work this out. I promise. "

Michael stopped and turned around. He was smiling, but it was a sad smile.

"Gene, I promise I will not do anything stupid."

13

When Betty returned with the kids, she lingered in the living room for a couple of minutes, and then headed into the kitchen to fix dinner. When Gene joined her she said, "So Michael was here?"

"How do you know?"

"I could smell that cologne. He always puts on too much."

They would talk after dinner when the kids were watching TV. The talk continued after the children went to bed.

Betty suggested that there might still be something unresolved between Michael and herself, but mostly she was alarmed about the gun. Clearly, Michael was trying to send a message, though even *he* probably wasn't sure what it was.

Gene said that maybe *he* was a big part of the problem: "I know that your problems with him go way back, but then this rich, old white guy arrived on the scene and stole his family away from him. No, he never said any of that, but it's not an unreasonable view—at least from Michael's perspective. And yet he freely admitted how badly he had treated you."

"Gene, what are you trying to say?"

"Well, let me put it *this* way. If something happened, if Michael used that gun, then a lot of that would be on me. Deep, deep down, you and I know that if I had not been with you, it never would have come to this."

"Are you breaking up with me?"

"Look, Betty. What we have is great! I've never been happier in my life. But Michael's visit has kind of rearranged things. If I stay, we could no longer be the way we were."

"Gene, you know that my children are the most important thing to me."

"Of course."

"If anything happened…"

"I know, honey. I know." He embraced her. They were both crying.

"Could you just keep holding me?"

He did.

A few hours later, after the kids left for school, she picked up the phone and called Michael.

14

Two months later, Gene and I had dinner at one of our favorite restaurants in Brooklyn Heights. We mostly reminisced about old times. Then he abruptly changed the subject.

"Steve, have you ever tried Internet dating?"

"No, I like to meet women face-to-face."

"You should try it! There's this woman I've been e-mailing. We've fallen in love with each other."

"And you've never actually met?"

"No, but I've booked a flight and I'm going to meet her in two weeks."

"Gene, where does she live? *China?*"

"Yes, as a matter of fact!"

FORTUNE COOKIES

So, what's the deal with Chinese fortune cookies? You know how they sometimes *do* accurately describe you or your future:

People are naturally attracted to you.

A dream you have will come true.

The greatest risk is not taking one.

Is the waiter playing a joke on us by hand-picking our fortunes? Or, does he just dip into a large box of cookies, and distribute them randomly?

Linda and I have been eating at an old-style Cantonese restaurant for years. One evening, when "Mike," our regular waiter, gave us our cookies, she asked him what the deal was.

"Mike, Garret and I are curious about the fortune cookies."

"Ah ha! You want to learn 'big secret.'"

"Yeah, Mike," I said. "Do you know what the fortunes are, and then give us the fortunes that you think we're hoping for?"

"So sorry, Garret. If I tell you, it would no longer be 'big secret.'" And before either of us could think of a clever reply, he rushed off to a man who was signaling for his check.

Linda and I just looked at each other and rolled our eyes.

"Do you think he's hiding something?"

"I don't have a clue, Linda. It's really hard to know when he's joking."

We opened our cookies and read our fortunes out loud. Mine was, "If you have something good in your life, don't let it go." Linda's was, "A new voyage will fill your life with untold memories."

"I think I should ask Mike for another cookie."

"Why's that?"

"I've used up all my vacation time, and I even owe the company a couple of weeks."

Linda and I have a comfortable relationship. We probably look like we've been married for maybe five or six years, and no longer have to go through the constant hand-holding, eye-gazing, affectionate little moves of couples just falling in love.

Yeah, we'd *been* there *done* that back in high school. Linda was my first love, and I'd like to think that just maybe I was hers too. But neither of us ever said the "L" word, and we never talked about getting married. We broke up amicably after high school, and went to different out-of-town colleges. Since then, although we were both living in the city, it seemed that either *she* was seeing someone or *I* was.

Over the years we even went out on a few double dates, which we both agreed was just too weird. So if anyone asked, "What's up with you two?" we'd probably describe ourselves as friends without benefits.

Linda must have noticed my faraway look.

"Garret, you wanna hear a funny story?"

"Sure."

"Do you remember my friend, Janet?"

"Vaguely."

"When we were in middle school, she was one of my best friends. Her parents had divorced when Janet was very young, and she would see her father every weekend."

"Wait! Don't tell me, Linda: He took her for Chinese food every Sunday."

"Of course he did!"

"I wonder if it was at this restaurant."

"No, it was a place in my old neighborhood. Anyway, they always ordered the same dishes and probably had the same waiter."

"Yeah?"

162

"So it was Janet's eighteenth birthday. Her father gave her a beautiful silver necklace with turquoise beads. And then the waiter brought the fortune cookies."

"Linda, something tells me that you're about to let me in on the 'big secret.'"

"Are you ready for this?"

"Sure."

"Janet cracked open her cookie. When she saw her fortune, she actually screamed so loud that everyone in the restaurant stopped eating and stared at her."

"What was her fortune?"

"Garret, her fortune said—and I quote—'How can you eat this shit?'"

"It actually *said* that?"

"True story!"

A year or so later, Linda and I were finishing our meal at the same restaurant. Linda had just returned from Boston, where she had been living with a guy. Things had not worked out, and she was very down on herself. She kept repeating, "How could I be so stupid?"

Even Mike sensed that something was off, so he held his banter to a minimum. We got through the meal just fine, mainly by avoiding any talk about her "relationship."

Finally, Mike brought the fortune cookies. Without a word, he placed ten cellophane packets in front of Linda. He smiled at her and then quickly walked off.

Linda looked at me and I just shrugged. Clearly, I had no idea what was going on.

"Look, Garret, the packets are numbered."

"Are you sure?"

"Look for yourself."

Indeed, they were numbered one through ten.

She broke open the first fortune cookie. I watched her face. She kind of frowned. Then she began to smile. And soon she was laughing.

Linda handed me the strip of paper. It read, "Linda, you think you're pretty smart."

163

Now we were *both* laughing. Then she opened the second cookie. Her fortune read, "So you were washing your clothes in a laundromat and you met this guy, Jason."

She was laughing harder as she handed it to me.

Her third fortune: "Half an hour after your clothes were dry, you were in the sack with this guy."

Cookie 4: He convinced you to give up your job and your apartment and move to Boston.

Cookie 5: Some things are not as they first appear.

Cookie 6: He was not that smart.

Cookie 7: He refused to eat Chinese food.

Cookie 8: The schmuck is thirty-four and still supported by his parents.

Cookie 9: A new voyage will fill your life with untold memories.

She didn't break open the last cookie. I knew enough to remain silent. She would do it when she was ready.

She drew a deep breath. She was ready for her tenth fortune. She opened the cookie, and then looked at her last fortune. She began to cry. Mike was approaching our table, but he stopped abruptly, and then fled back into the kitchen.

Finally, she wiped away her tears, and began mouthing a single word over and over, while nodding quite emphatically.

What did her tenth fortune say? So sorry, but it's a "big secret."

MY RICH UNCLE

1

I remember my parents referring to Uncle Bill as "a confirmed bachelor." Now, a bachelor was an unmarried man. But what, exactly, was a *confirmed* bachelor?

I heard my parents and some of my aunts and uncles, call old women—usually in their forties or fifties—"spinsters." So, I thought there has to be some connection between the confirmed bachelors and the spinsters.

I pretty much figured it out by the time of my *own* confirmation. My mother bought me a beautiful dress, and the whole family went to church where Father James presided over the ceremony. So, I concluded that when unmarried men reached the age of forty—or maybe it was fifty—they bought a nice suit and went to church to be confirmed.

But what about the spinsters? Was there a confirmation ceremony for them, too? I discussed this with my friend, Rosemary. She told me that if a woman was not married by her fortieth birthday, she had to become a nun.

I thought about this, but quickly realized that Rosemary must have been given the wrong information. There were plenty of spinsters walking around, and some of them were clearly *not* nuns. Rosemary and I concluded that the ones who did not become nuns must have had secret confirmation ceremonies which, of course, made them "confirmed spinsters."

2

Uncle Bill was twenty-five years older than my mother. One day I asked her if he was *really* her brother.

"That's an excellent question, Eileen. Bill is actually my *half*-brother. Do you know what a half-brother is?"

"Mom, I don't have a clue."

"Bill and I have the same father, but different mothers."

"How come?"

"Well, Bill's mother died. Her name was Mary."

"When did she die?"

"She died when Bill was about twelve."

"*Then* what happened?"

"A few years later, Bill's father married Grandma Helen."

"And then *you* were born!"

"Yes. And that makes Bill my half-brother."

"So then, he's my *half*-uncle."

"Correct."

"So why does he say he's my uncle if he's only my *half*-uncle?"

"That's because he loves you very much."

3

When I was about four, Uncle Bill would play *Chutes and Ladders* and *Uno* with me. As I remember, he was pretty good for a confirmed bachelor, and was even able beat me a few times. But he often admitted that I was a far better player than he was.

One day, he asked me what I wanted to be.

"A *lawyer!*"

He seemed surprised.

"Why a lawyer?"

"I want to help poor people."

"Eileen, that is truly admirable."

"Uncle Bill, I know it kind of means 'good,' but what does admirable actually mean?"

"It means, honey, even *better* than good.

"Eileen, I know you are already eight years old, but don't you think that's a little young to decide on your life's work? And how do lawyers help poor people?"

"There was a very poor family that lived just down the block from us. Their landlord threw all their stuff out on the street. They had to go to a homeless shelter."

"How awful!"

"Well, Uncle Bill, if I was a lawyer, I would have gone to court and stopped that landlord from doing that. And the mother had just had another baby."

"You know something, honey? If you want to be a lawyer—and to help poor people—then I'm sure that you will someday be a really fine lawyer."

4

A few years later, Uncle Bill came over for dinner. My mom had made his favorite dish, corned beef and cabbage. He always used to kid that you had to be careful not to eat too much of the cabbage or not enough corned beef.

He was wearing a jacket I had seen many times before. My dad often teased him about how old it was. Finally, Uncle Bill seemed to take offense.

"I'll have you know that this jacket was *custom* made!"

"I'm sure it was," said my mom. "But for *whom*?"

My parents roared with laughter. Then, a few seconds later, I finally got it and started laughing too. The laughter was contagious, and even Uncle Bill couldn't stop himself.

5

My parents and my other aunts and uncles were divided on this question: Was Uncle Bill rich or was he poor?

Aunt Rose made the best case that he was rich:

"First of all, he has worked in the Post Office for over forty years, and he's still going strong. True, the pay is not great, but everyone knows what a tightwad he is. He lives in a small rent-stabilized apartment, and we all know how much he spends on clothes. I'll bet he's got hundreds of thousands squirreled away."

Then, Uncle Paddy argued the opposite:

"We all know about Bill's devotion to the Catholic Workers' organization. Now I've got nothing against them— they do very good work for the poor—but they also make all their members take a vow of poverty. I happen to know personally that he hands over almost his entire paycheck every week."

"That shows how much *you* know, Paddy" piped up my dad. The Post Office pays their employees every *two* weeks."

"Fine," said Uncle Paddy. "So then he gets to give 'em *twice* as much!"

I sat there listening, and even though I had heard Uncle Bill talk occasionally about *the Catholic Worker*, all I knew about them was that they helped the poor.

The next time Uncle Bill came over, I asked him to tell me what this group actually *did* to help the poor.

"Uncle Bill, do you work for *The Catholic Worker*?"

"Sort of. I do volunteer work for them. Not for them, but for the organization itself. They have a couple of buildings near the Bowery, which is a street in the City. But my regular job is in the Post Office sorting mail."

"Tell me about the Catholic Worker."

"It's a kind of community, a community where everyone shares. If someone is hungry, that person is fed. If someone has no clothes, that person is given clothes. And the homeless are given a place to sleep."

"Isn't that like a homeless shelter?"

"In a way it is. But we give out of love. In our "houses of hospitality," we are all the same. In a sense, we're all poor. But you could also say we are all rich. That's because we are a sharing community."

"Can I come to see it?"

"Of course! But I think it would be best if you came with your parents."

168

6

I went to Uncle Bill's community many times, usually helping to serve meals, and often just sitting around talking with whoever was there. Going there strengthened my resolve to become a lawyer. I really got to know poverty almost firsthand.

Before going to law school, I still needed to attend college. Even if I had wanted to go to an out-of-town school, my parents would not have been able to afford to send me. And law school would be still another financial burden.

But Uncle Bill remained very encouraging. He often said that if I *really* wanted to be a lawyer, then I *could* become one.

I remember the family dispute about whether Uncle Bill was rich or poor. I knew that he certainly *did* contribute a lot to the Catholic Worker community—in time *and* money.

When I was ready to apply to law schools, Uncle Bill was even more direct: "If you *really* want to go, you can *do* it. I may be just half an uncle, but I have full faith in my niece. "

Was there a hidden message? Was there a hint that if I fully committed to going, he would help pay the tuition? That is, if he actually *had* the money.

The only way I managed to get through the first year was to live at home and take out huge student loans. I still came to the "house of hospitality" whenever I could. Uncle Bill had finally retired from the Post Office, but only because his health was failing.

Whenever he saw me, he would address me as Esquire Eileen. And whenever I mentioned my financial woes, he observed, "You made it *this* far; I know you'll make it all the way."

By the beginning of the third and final year, I doubted that I would ever be able to pay off my loans—especially since I would never earn very much representing the poor. But I had to admit that Uncle Bill had been right after all. I certainly *could* make it through law school, and even do it on my own.

A few months later, Uncle Bill passed away. When we visited the funeral home, I tried to hold back my tears. But when I looked in the coffin, I completely lost it. My parents put their arms around me. Then they led me away.

"Did you see what he was wearing?"

Of course they did. It was his custom-made jacket.

A week later, Uncle Bill's lawyer asked us to come to her office. Surprisingly, none of the other family members were there. It turned out that Uncle Paddy had been right. Uncle Bill *had* given most of his paycheck to the Catholic Worker Movement.

Then his lawyer addressed me. "You must *know* how proud you made your uncle. You were the only family member who visited the 'house of hospitality.' You went almost every week since you were in middle school."

She stopped talking. We waited. Was that *it*?

Then she smiled, cleared her throat, and continued.

"A few years ago, your uncle changed his will. He made arrangements to pay off all your student loans."

7

Most people use money as a proxy for success and even happiness. By that standard, Uncle Bill was not a rich man.

Since I was a little girl, he recognized a kindred spirit, and he shared with me the joy of giving to others. And for that, I will be forever grateful. He was indeed my rich uncle.

THE EXISTENTIAL POSSIBILITY

SCENE 1

It's a late fall afternoon. The sunlight streams through the living room windows of an apartment on the Upper West Side of Manhattan. A man in his early thirties sits on the couch. A woman a few years younger sits opposite him in a rocker.

BILL: When will he be here?

JEAN: Maybe a half an hour.

BILL: He's got a car?

JEAN: Whadda yuh think? Look at all this stuff.

BILL: I mean he lives here in the city and he's got a car?

JEAN: He needs it for work.

BILL: He's got a business?

JEAN: Come-*on*, Billy, *You* don't have to make like the Spanish Inquisition.

BILL: Just making conversation.

JEAN: Some conversation!

BILL: Look, what I'm saying is that it's still not too late.

JEAN: Billy, we've been through this a million times already. In thirty minutes I'm leaving here. That's it! And I don't like you even *being* here.

BILL: I *live* here.

JEAN: Yeah, but you don't have to sit here and turn this thing into a funeral.

BILL: My own.

JEAN: Well, you don't have to. And don't make out like things are so tragic... Look, we tried. We both tried.... And... and... it just didn't work out.

BILL: It *could* have worked out. It could of if we just gave it more time.

JEAN: Let me tell you something. My life is made up of time. And every day living here with you is one more day out of my life.

BILL: But it's only been three months!

JEAN: Ninety-six days, to be exact. But who's counting?

BILL: Jeannie! Jeannie! I know that you still care about me—

JEAN: Sure I care about you. And I always *will* care. It's just that some things are meant to be. And others....

BILL: We were one of the others.

JEAN: That's not what I said.

BILL: No, I said it *for* you.

JEAN: Come-*on*, Billy. Look, it's *over*. I'm sorry to have to be so blunt. Now don't take things any more awkward than they already are.

BILL: Don't worry. They can't be much more awkward than this.

JEAN: Let's not press our luck.

BILL: OK, OK. Look, I'm sorry that I started in on you. I guess it's kind of hard to move and live with someone else. That's two of life's crises in one. At least I don't have to move. I just have to go through one crisis— the loss of a loved one.

JEAN: Please, Billy. Let's dispense with the pathos.

BILL: Do you think you would've stayed if I had said it was OK to see other guys?

JEAN: Come on, can't you just *drop* it?

BILL: Just answer me *that* one. I've really been tortured by whether or not you would've stayed.

JEAN: Truthfully?

BILL: Even if it hurts.

172

JEAN: If you had said, "I love you, but I can't stand in your way," I probably would have ended up doing just about the same as I did.

BILL: So it really didn't make any difference.

JEAN: I didn't *say* that! When you told me that you wouldn't let me, you really did two things. First, you were making an ownership claim.

BILL: Ownership! I told you that I loved you and that it would really hurt me if you went out looking for other guys.

JEAN: But don't you see that that just put boundaries around me? You are telling me what I *could* do and what I *couldn't* do.

BILL: I just said it would *hurt* me.

JEAN: Don't *hurt* me translates to don't *do* it. It might not be a direct order, but it has the same effect. Anyway, when you did this to me, you made an ownership claim. But you also placed a tremendous inhibition on my freedom. You inhibited my freedom to imagine being with someone else.

BILL: So you wanted to be with someone else?

JEAN: Not necessarily. I wasn't unhappy with you. But I wanted to be free to just imagine being with someone else. What was that corny Glen Campbell song?

BILL: "The Dreams of the Everyday Housewife."

JEAN: Right!

BILL: So you didn't want to actually *do* anything? You just wanted to dream about it?

JEAN: Maybe I kinda wanted to do something. I don't know. What I'm saying is that you tried to take away even my dreams.

BILL: Any way you look at it, you weren't happy with me. You were just looking for a way to break up.

JEAN: If I wanted to break up with you, I wouldn't have needed any excuses. And stop trying to make me out to be the villain.

BILL: So, *I'm* the villain!

173

JEAN: Nobody's the villain. It just didn't work out is all.

BILL: Well, *I* tried. And *I* didn't want to *see* anyone else.

JEAN: I think you're missing the whole point. I wanted to be free. Free to imagine. Free to explore. Free to be myself.

BILL: And all I did was inhibit you.

JEAN: Well, frankly, yes. I know you didn't mean to.

BILL: All I wanted was to love you. Is *that* such a crime?

JEAN: Oh, Billy, stop being so dramatic. I'm not really blaming you.

BILL: Could of fooled me.

JEAN: What I'm trying to say is that you meant well, but the *effect* of what you did was inhibiting. Being loved by you was so nice and secure. But so final! And after only couple of months. You just kept rushing things.

BILL: You don't rush something like love. I wasn't in a hurry to be in love with you. It just happened. Look—I'm sorry I didn't mean to fall in love with you so fast. And I'm sorry it inhibited you.

JEAN: No need to get sarcastic... Now I'm going to try to explain this to you one more time. *(pause about 5 seconds)* Okay... Now there we were living together a couple of months. And you were telling me you loved me. And you wanted me to say it back.

BILL: You didn't *have* to. I didn't make it conditional.

JEAN: No, but you wanted me to.

BILL: OK! I plead guilty!

JEAN: You damn well plead guilty! And you have no idea how much pressure that put me under. Here's this guy telling me how much he loved me and I'm thinking—do I love *him*?

BILL: I shouldn't have said anything?

JEAN: Well, it kinda got me thinking. I mean, I didn't *think* I was in love. Maybe I *could* be, some day. But now? No, I didn't *think* so. Then I said to myself—if I'm not in love with *this* guy, then maybe I could fall in love with someone else.

174

BILL: So you wanted to find someone else.

JEAN: No—not find. Not even *look* for. No, more like—be open to the possibility. I think they call that the existential possibility.

BILL: OK, so this guy who's going to ring our bell any second now—*he's* your existential possibility? But isn't it possible you could do still better? Isn't it possible that there's someone else floating around out there who is your *ultimate* existential possibility?

JEAN: I suppose there is.

BILL: Then why move in with *this* guy?

JEAN: Because you have to take chances.

BILL: Then why not take a chance with me?

JEAN: Because, quite frankly, Billy, Hank is pretty damn close to my existential possibility. He's what I would have filled in on the computer dating form.

BILL: And how would I have ranked on that form?

JEAN: Billy, don't ask me something like that. It's not better or worse. It's what's good for *me*. Probably most women would rank you ahead of Hank.

BILL: That and a token will get me on the subway.

JEAN: Look, this is getting pretty inane. Let's drop this whole thing, shall we?

SCENE 2

Same room a half hour later. The sun has gone down and the last glow of twilight leaves the room in three-quarter darkness. Jean and Bill have remained seated.

BILL: Maybe you better call him.

JEAN: No, if there was any problem he would have called.

BILL: Look, Jeannie, I'm really sorry.

JEAN: Sorry? About what? That he's half an hour late?

BILL: OK, have it *your* way.

JEAN: What's *that's* supposed to mean?

BILL: Nothing... nothing. Anyway, where did you say you'll be living? Just a few blocks from here?

175

JEAN: I *wrote* out the address and phone number. You've got it on the night table!

BILL: Now Jeannie, you don't have to jump down my throat. *You're* the one who's leaving me.

JEAN: Ah Billie, I'm sorry. I guess I *am* getting nervous.

BILL: Maybe you *should* call him.

JEAN: Oh, I don't know. If I do, I'll just look stupid.

BILL: I hate to say this, but maybe something happened to him. Maybe you'd better check. New York didn't get its reputation for nothing.

JEAN: I think I'll wait another few minutes. If it's nothing, I'll have just made a damn fool of myself.

BILL: Join the club.

JEAN: I'll say *one* thing for you. You sure don't mind laughing at yourself. Yuh know? I always liked that!

BILL: Well, that's a start!

JEAN: I'm afraid it's a little too late for that.

BILL: It's never too late.

JEAN: Well, I think it's late enough for me to ring his number. *(She picks up the phone and dials... She waits, holding the phone slightly away from her ear... Finally, she puts the phone down.)*

BILL: Nobody home?

JEAN: He must be on the way over.

BILL: Sure. He's probably double-parking in front of our house right now.

JEAN: Are you sure the bell is working?

BILL: It was last night.

JEAN: Last night?

BILL: Yeah, I ordered some Chinese food from Wong's Palace. Spare ribs, pork fried rice, and sweet and sour chicken. Have you ever had sweet and sour chicken? It's really good.

JEAN: You had someone up here? In *our* bed?

BILL: No offense, honey, but I really didn't think you'd mind, seeing as you wouldn't be using *our* bed last night. Or tonight for that matter.

176

JEAN: I just find that pretty tacky. In *our* bed and all. Couldn't you wait one more night? Why didn't you stay at *her* apartment?

BILL: Her mother isn't that liberated.

JEAN: She lives with her *mother?* I was out of my parents' house before I was nineteen!

BILL: Well, then, she still has a little time.

JEAN: How old *is* this girl?

BILL: I think she just had a birthday. So she must be sixteen.

JEAN: I don't *believe* this! Is she really sixteen?

BILL: Well, how old is this Hank?

JEAN: Hank happens to be thirty-six years old.

BILL: Maybe we can fix him up with Tracy.

JEAN: Come clean, Bill. Is she really sixteen years old?

BILL: I'm not at liberty to say. Only a scoundrel would give away a woman's age.

JEAN: Only a scoundrel would seduce a sixteen-year-old girl.

BILL: What can I tell you? Younger women find me attractive.

JEAN: Younger children, you mean!

BILL: If the older ones no longer like you, there's only one other alternative. Anyway, maybe you better give old Hank another call.

JEAN: I don't want to appear anxious.

BILL: Don't worry. The guy's nearly an hour late. He should have called *you!*

JEAN: You're right! *(She picks up the phone and dials and waits about twenty seconds.)* Hello, Hank?...Are you all right....Hank?... What's the matter? *(She waits about twenty seconds.)* No... it's okay. *(She waits about ten seconds.)* You're....no, no, I...I...understand. *(She hangs up the phone. Bill slowly gets up and walks over to her. He puts his arms around her as she cries gently.)*

SCENE 3

It's completely dark outside. A corner lamp partially illuminates the room. Jean lies on the couch with her head resting on Bill's lap.

177

BILL: Do you want to tell me what he said?

JEAN: Not really.

BILL: I guess it would be kind of redundant to tell you that I still love you.

JEAN: I know.

BILL: Does all this mean he wasn't your existential possibility, after all?

JEAN: I guess not. And I certainly wasn't his. I mean, of all the stupid excuses I've heard people come up with—

BILL: This one took the cake.

JEAN: Yeah, something like that. I mean, would you believe that his ex-girlfriend decided she wanted to move back in with him?

BILL: Well,...actually—

JEAN: Never mind! You *would* see the irony!

BILL: And to think that little Tracy would leave her mother for that same man. Why he's twenty years older than her.

JEAN: What are you *talking* about?

BILL: Ah, how quickly we forget. Tracy, you know, the little girl who shared Chinese food with me last night?

JEAN : Tracy and Hank? He's more than twice her age! *Damn it,* Bill! Do you have to turn everything into a joke?

BILL: OK, OK! I promise! So, what really happened with poor old Hank?

JEAN: That's all he said. That she was moving back in and that he should have called me. How he hated so much to give bad news. That he just couldn't bring himself to call.

BILL: So he let you pack up all your stuff and sit here waiting because he didn't have the guts to tell you.

JEAN: Now, Bill, no need for *you* to get upset. It was I who was left standing there like an idiot. But what the hell. At least I found out what a wimp that guy was *before* I moved in with him.

BILL: Yeah, with me it took you at least a month *after* you moved in here.

JEAN: Maybe I *still* didn't find out.

BILL: Meaning what?

JEAN: Meaning if you can keep your mouth shut at the right times, maybe we can give it another try.

BILL: *Really?* No more existential possibilities?

JEAN: Well, let's just say there may be one I'd like to check out over the next sixty or seventy years.

BILL: Sixty or seventy years?

JEAN: Uh huh.

BILL: Uh huh?

JEAN: Yeah. If you could tell me just one thing I've been a little curious about?

BILL: What's that?

JEAN: Was she really only sixteen?

BILL: We--e---e----e----l---l---l---l. Maybe.... She was really....seventeen.... or eighteen.

FINAL CURTAIN

JOHN THE PLUMBER

1

My Uncle Harry sent his three sons to Ivy League colleges. For years, that's all he ever wanted to talk about. Often, he would sum it all up by observing that "They ain't no dummies."

I used to think that by inference, maybe he meant that I was a dummy. After all, I went to Queens College and probably would not have been admitted to any of the Ivy League schools even if my parents could have afforded to send me.

But in recent years, Uncle Harry's tune has changed. "I wish the three of 'em became plumbers. Those guys make a good living."

Harry's boys had great aspirations. Marty was living in LA, trying to break in as a screenwriter. Any day now, he expected someone to option one of his scripts. Jerry was a pretty good violinist, but he was still trying to catch on with a municipal orchestra. Which one? *Any* one of them.

But the son who pissed off Harry the most was Barry, who was still chasing *his* dream—to be a professional baseball player. Now, in fairness, most of the boys in our neighborhood had wanted to play for the Mets or the Yankees. But by the age of eight or ten, they began dreaming of more realistic careers. Barry was twenty-nine years old and still slept with his baseball glove under his pillow.

"Yeah," cracked Uncle Harry. "Just in case he dreamed that Bryce Harper hit a fly ball to him." Harry loved all of his jokes, but *that* one never failed to crack him up.

Marty and Jerry certainly had some talent, but Barry had struck out—literally and figuratively—at every level above Little League, where everyone was given a chance to play.

In pick-up games in Cunningham Park, he was picked last—if at all. At Newtown High School, on the day that tryouts were held, the coach took Barry aside and told him that he was wasting his time—and everybody else's.

At Brown, the coach was even more frank. "Barry, I don't want you to take this the wrong way, but your chances of making this team—or any other college, high school, or Little League team is about as good as Saddam Hussein's being elected president of Israel."

"But that's not a good analogy," argued Barry. "Saddam Hussein has been dead for years."

"*Think* about it, son! Now get out of here and let me get back to work."

Ten years later, Barry was in Israel, trying out for teams in their semi-professional summer league.

"So Kaplan," asked one of the general managers, "you're Jewish, right?"

"Right."

"Are you thinking of making *Aliyah?*" (Moving to Israel and becoming a citizen)

"Maybe."

"*Great!* After you've made *Aliyah* and are ready to do your military service, come back and we can talk."

"About baseball?"

"What kind of baseball? I work full-time as a recruiter for the Israeli Defense Force. The ball club gig is just summers."

At that moment, it finally dawned on Barry, that just maybe, he would not be the second coming of Mickey Mantle.

2

Uncle Harry often complained that at least one of his three sons was living at home. The boys kind of alternated. A few weeks before Marty moved to LA, Jerry and his wife moved back in. He needed to schedule auditions with several symphony orchestras throughout the Midwest, buy a car, and go from one city to the next until he landed a spot.

Barry was in and out of the house, still following his impossible dream. And Uncle Harry was growing more and more cynical.

"We never shoulda sent the three of 'em to those damn Ivy League colleges. All I got tuh show for it is them damn student loan bills. If I wasn't payin' em off myself, my boys would all be in debtors' prison."

More and more he would lament they're never having become plumbers. "Those guys make a real living. An' lemme ask yuh: Yuh ever hear of a thirty-year-old plumber living with his parents?"

My answer was, "No, but I didn't *know* any plumbers.

Then I met John.

3

My friend, Grace, had been seeing someone and asked if I wanted to go double.

"Sure," but I'm not going out with anyone special right now.

"Mike has this friend who really *is* special. I promise you'll like him. In fact, I predict you'll marry him."

"*Tell* me about him."

"What's there to *tell?* When the two of you see each other, you'll click. Or not. Either way, the four of us will have a great time."

"OK, what have I got to lose?"

4

The four of us would meet in front of a Korean restaurant on Queens Boulevard in Middle Village. John would pick me up. We could walk to the restaurant from my house.

Grace still talks about that night. She and Mike arrived at the restaurant first. It was just getting dark, and in the distance they saw a couple stumbling down the street. They were so drunk they could barely walk. They kept stopping and looked as though they were supporting each other.

"Pretty early to be *that* drunk," observed Mike.

"Yeah, you can say *that* again. How about a little bet which one falls down on the sidewalk first?"

"Or gets sick," he added.

A few seconds later Grace blurted out: "Holy *shit*! It's *them*!"

"And they're *not* drunk! They're making out!"

It took another couple of minutes for me and John to make our way to the restaurant.

"Well," said Mike, "I see that you two have managed to get acquainted."

5

John never went to college. He came from a solid blue-collar family. His father had had a small construction contracting business and cherished his independence.

"I'm the boss," he loved to say. "Nobody bosses *me!*"

"That's right, Freddie. And nobody pays you a steady salary either," chipped in his wife, Gail.

"OK, *enough* already!"

"Freddie, how many times have you complained about how your customers keep promising to pay you?"

"Yeah, but they're always good for the money."

"Sure they are! But *when*?"

"John," his father would say, "whatever you do, don't marry a nag."

At that point, John's mother would just laugh, and then leave the room.

John's father would often remind him: "You put your tools in three separate boxes, so you don't mix them up. Your electrical tools go in one box. Your carpentry tools go in another box. And your plumbing tools go in a third box."

From the time John was about seven, he would always ask: "Where do you keep the three boxes?"

"In my vehicle."

"Did anyone ever steal your tools?"

"Yes. But then I solved that problem."

John knew the story by heart, but he also knew his father loved telling it.

"How did you stop them from stealing your tools?"

"I bought a hearse."

"What's a hearse, dad?"

"It's a vehicle that undertakers use to transport dead bodies to the cemetery."

John knew his next line by heart.

"Why didn't they steal your tools from the hearse?"

"Because I kept them in the coffin. Thieves were afraid to break in because they could see the coffin through the window."

"So why did *that* stop them?"

"*Think* about it, son."

John would wait a few seconds and then burst out laughing. And his dad joined in. Soon his mother yelled from the next room.

"Knock it off, you two! You're making such a racket, you'll wake up the dead!"

Then they heard *her* start laughing. The whole routine had become a family joke.

6

Growing up, John knew he wouldn't follow his father's footsteps. That is, he could never be a contractor. He heard too many stories about hammering shingles onto rooves, and of guys falling off ladders. By the time he was twelve, he had settled upon becoming a plumber.

Although his dad made noises about his son wimping out, John knew that he was actually very pleased. After all, being a plumber was the next best thing next to being a contractor, and as Freddie was forced to admit, John would never have to worry about keeping his tools separated.

When John and I met, he had his own plumbing business and had a couple of guys working for him. When Uncle Harry met him, I thought he was going to wet his pants. *This* was the guy who should have been his son.

Did I mention that John was the most attractive guy I ever met? And as luck would have it, he felt the same about me.

So what were we waiting for? We got married six months after we met. And we managed to find a small house in the neighborhood that we actually could afford.

7

The only problem we had was politics. I was a very liberal Democrat and John was pretty conservative. Luckily, our differences were not over social issues, but bread-and-butter economic issues.

John fell for the old Republican line of the government making the poor dependent by keeping them on dole, and he felt that immigrants—especially *illegal* immigrants—were taking jobs away from Americans.

Then, of course, there were the old Republican standbys— too many people receiving government handouts like food stamps, Medicaid, and welfare. Why should we be paying high taxes to support all these people who didn't want to work?

Miraculously, we never really argued. We just agreed to disagree. Besides, we had a set of very demanding two-year-old twins, Tina and Tommy, to keep us on the straight and narrow.

Still, when Donald Trump was elected, it was all we could do to keep our political differences from boiling over. And then, one evening, Grace and I went for a walk, and everything changed.

John was home getting the twins ready for bed. When Grace asked how things we going with John, I told her. It was Trump's being right about *this* and Trump's being right about *that*. If I didn't love the bastard so much, I would have hauled off and belted him.

Grace let me rant for a while. Just as I was beginning to calm down, we saw a commotion in front of a run-down three-story apartment house. There were rumors around the neighborhood that it was filled with squatters who had taken over what had been an abandoned building. I remember seeing it fenced off and boarded up just a few weeks before.

As we approached, there was a crowd of people standing in front of the house. A couple of women, one holding a baby, begged us to help them. The basement was flooding. It was hard to understand them because they both had thick accents and were crying.

"Call John," said Grace.

He picked up on the second ring.

"Is everything alright?"

I told him what was going on. In a very calm voice, he explained exactly what to do. I asked him to stay on the line while I followed his instructions.

We went down to the basement. There was a stream of water pouring out of a pipe. John asked me where we were—at the front or at the back of the building?

The back. He said to walk to the front. Grace and I splashed through the water, which was almost up to our knees.

John asked if we had reached the front yet. Almost. Then, yes, we were at the front.

"OK, now look for an overhead pipe running the length of the basement."

"It's hard to see. It's dark down here."

"That's alright. Just reach up to the ceiling and feel for the pipe."

I told Grace what he said and we both searched for the pipe.

"I found it!" yelled Grace.

John heard her.

"OK, I want the two of you to feel along the pipe. There should be a valve. Let me know when you locate it."

It took us about thirty seconds.

"*Got* it!"

"Great! Now see if you can turn it clockwise."

I tried, but it was stuck.

"Can you move it?" he asked.

I told him I couldn't.

187

"OK, see if you can find a piece of metal or a piece of wood. The valve is probably rusted and may need just a couple of knocks to loosen it up."

I told Grace to look around and she found a broom. I started banging it against the valve.

John could actually hear the clanging.

"Just tap it. Pretend you're cousin Barry, trying out for the Mets."

That broke the tension for me. John knew I was smiling.

When I tried to turn the valve, it gave very slightly. I hit the valve some more, and soon, I was able to turn it about a quarter of an inch at a time.

Soon I could hear the stream of water losing some of its force. I kept at it until there was barely a trickle. The people in the basement started to cheer.

"Honey," said John, a bit sardonically, "I think those people are about to award you a medal for heroism."

"I don't *think* so. Grace and I are soaked. We don't look too heroic just now."

"Well, you're *my* hero."

"John, I need to tell you something. I think this building is filled with illegal immigrants. In fact, I'm pretty sure. They probably didn't call the Fire Department because they were afraid they might get deported."

"Honey, listen to me: No one's getting deported."

"John…"

"Look, just come home and take the twins off my hands. I'll grab my tools and go over there and see what I can do."

I didn't say anything. After several seconds, I heard John's panicked voice: "Are you still *there?*"

"John, I need to tell you something."

"OK."

"Remember when we met?"

"Are you kidding?"

"Remember how happy we were?"

"Sure."

"Well, tonight you've made me even happier."

HUMPERS IN HEAVEN

1

August 1, 1960

The three of them are squeezed into the front seat of Mike's car. Actually, the car belongs to Mike's father, but why get technical? It's a two-tone green, 1952 De Soto.

Kevin has blue eyes, a nice smile, he's tall, and is still filling out. Very soon all the girls will be falling in love with him. Mike's got a d.a. (duck's ass) haircut, but his hair is really too curly to wear that way. So, he has about half a pound of grease in it. That's a bit much, even for 1960. Vinnie's short, wiry, and usually has this half-puzzled look. He has big brown eyes and is actually kind of nice looking.

They're headed for the City. When someone asks to see some I.D., they'll flash their newly acquired draft cards. Mike and Vinnie turned 18 in May, and Kevin did just last week.

"So, Kev," says Mike, "do yuh have any idea where we're headed?"

"No, you guys said it was supposed to be some kind of birthday surprise."

"Or maybe, kind of an initiation," said Vinnie.

"We're taking yuh to a really great place. You'll *love* it, Kev.

"I dunno, Mike. I just got a couple of bucks with me."

"Yuh money's no good tonight. Ain't that right, Vinne?"

"That's right, Mike. Kev, tonight yuh going to bust yuh cherry."

"Maybe yuh better count me out. I gotta get up early tomorrow."

"Too late tuh back out now, Kev. We're there," says Mike. They park and get out of the car. He takes Kevin by the arm.

"Vinnie, grab his other arm. Looks like we may have to drag him over there."

"OK, OK! Look, just tell me where we're going."

"Mike, you want to tell him or should I?"

"*You* tell him."

"OK, Kev. We are just a couple blocks away from one of the greatest entertainment spots in the city—"Humpers' Heaven."

"You mean you're taking me to a *prostitute*? What if I catch something? My old man... shit, my old man'll kill me. That's all I need. No... no—count me out!"

"Hold on a second! Mike, yuh better explain where we're going."

"Look Kevin, here's the deal. We're going to this dance hall. That's all it is. There are these women there who yuh dance with. Only yuh don't exactly dance. What yuh do is grind. Yuh know how to grind?"

"Sure."

"So yuh know what that kind of dancing is called?

"I forget."

"It's called *dry* humping."

"Wait a second, Mike. Are you saying..."

"Vinnie! I think the kid's finally catching on."

"So Kev, what we're going to be doing—yuh can call that '*wet* humping,'" adds Vinnie.

"Holy *shit*!"

"That's all you got to do. Just grind. It'll take yuh about ten seconds."

"Yuh mean tuh...?"

"That's right!"

"Shouldn't I put on something?"

"A bag?"

"Yeah. maybe we should stop in a drug store. I don't have any with me."

"Nah, yuh don't need nothing. What, do yuh expect to catch something through yuh pants?"

"Well won't my pants get stained? I can't go home like that."

"Don't worry. By the time yuh get home, it'll dry out. Ain't that right, Vinnie?"

"Well, I'm wearing my good pair of pants. What if my father sees the stains?"

"I'm telling yuh, yuh ain't got nothing to worry about," said Vinnie. They stop walking. "OK, look Kev. I worn these pants three or four times up there. Yuh see any stains?"

"No."

"One more thing, Kev," said Mike. "Just act cool. Yuh gotta pretend yer dancin', so make like yuh movin yuh feet. They got this rule that yuh have to dance. Maybe they're afraid a being raided by the police or something."

"There's this guy who walks around the dance floor with a wooden pointer," adds Vinnie. Yuh got to at least pretend yuh dancing. If yuh standing still too long, this guy taps yuh on the shoulder. Then yuh got to move yuh feet. And yuh have to start grinding all over again."

"Me, I like to get myself into a corner where I could keep an eye on that guy. I pick myself a good one an then I get to work. I never need more then two tickets—tops."

"When yuh finish," adds Mike, yuh go into the bathroom to clean up. There's all these guys in there tryin to wipe themselves off. There's even a guy selling paper towels. Let me tell yuh—I wish I made the money *that* guy makes!"

"Is that the place over there, Mike?"

"Yeah, where those two guys just went in."

"Right," said Vinnie. "Now just act real casual, Kev, and you'll come out alright—if yuh get my meaning."

"Ha, ha. If I wasn't scared shitless, I'd be laughing at this whole thing. I mean, we're paying money to rub up against some old whores."

"'*Old* whores', eh Mike? Wait till yuh get a load of some of them 'old whores.'"

"Yeah, that's rich. Yuh going to be eating those words. OK, Kev—Vinnie and I are going to buy some tickets and we'll be all set."

A minute later Mike hands Kevin four tickets. "OK, now look around for someone yuh like. Then ask her to dance. Yuh give her a ticket each time they change the record. Another record goes on maybe twenty seconds later. In between, just in case yuh deaf or something, they ring this cowbell. So now it's every man for himself. See yuh in the john in a couple of minutes."

"In a couple of *minutes?*"

"Sure, whatever. Look, Vinnie already got started."

"OK, I'll be alright. Let me just look around."

"Sure, but just remember what yuh here for. Yuh got to use them tickets. See yuh in the john."

"Right. I'll be in there as soon as I finish."

He looked around. At first it looked like a normal party. There were eighteen or twenty couples dancing and a bunch of guys leaning against the wall watching. He began to notice what was going in. And there was the man with the wooden pointer tapping a guy on the shoulder. Then the cowbell rang and some of the couples separated, while most of the guys handed tickets to the women they were with. A few guys went into the men's room. The next song came on.

And then he saw her. "Excuse me, would you like to dance?"

"Sure."

"What's your name?"

"Suzanne."

"That's nice."

"*What's* nice?"

"Your name."

"Thanks. Thanks a lot. What's *your* name?"

"Kevin."

"Irish?"

"Yeah, how'd you know?"

"Believe me, I *know*."

"Do you know a lot of Irish guys?"

"Sure. Thousands of 'em."

"Come here often?

"*What?*"

"I mean… er… this is my first time."

"I see."

"I'll tell you the truth. I'm kind of scared."

"I can see that too."

"You know what I'd *really* like?"

"Let me guess. You'd like to take me away from all this. In fact, you'd like to take me out on a date."

"How'd you know?

"Lucky guess."

"Will you?"

"I can't."

"Why not? You think I'm too young?"

"No, it's not that."

"Well, tell me why?"

"I just can't do it."

"Are you seeing someone? Do you have a boyfriend?"

"No, that's not it."

The record ends and then cowbell is rung. He hands her another ticket.

"I guess you just don't like me." They start dancing again.

"No, you're nice enough. Maybe nicer than anyone else who ever came in here. But we're not allowed to date the customers."

"This place has a lot of rules, doesn't it?"

"Yeah, a lot of rules. Just like the Church."

"Hey, you shouldn't say that."

"Why, is that another rule?"

"Sorry. I guess I shouldn't come in here and tell you how to run your life."

"Why *not*! That would be the least of my problems."

193

"Well, if they have this rule, why do you have to tell 'em if you go out with me?"

"You don't understand. If they found out, I'd get fired on the spot."

"You need the job?"

"What do *you* think?"

"I think you need the job."

"I think you're right."

"Are you allowed to keep dancing with the same guy?"

"That's what I'm here for."

"Would you keep dancing with me even if someone else wanted to?"

"As long as you've got the tickets."

"Well, I've still got two left."

"One." Just then the cowbell rings. He hands her the ticket. They start to dance.

"Could I have your phone number?"

"Kevin, you're really sweet. And I would even go out with you if I could. But you want me to lose my job?"

"No... Maybe...Oh, I don't know."

"My, aren't we getting possessive."

"Hey, don't *tease* me!"

"Sorry... occupational habit."

"Suzanne, would you believe me if I told you that I just want to hold you?"

"I'm starting to get the picture."

"Well, it's true. What I really want to do—more than anything else—is to go some place and just hold you."

"You're doing just fine right here."

"You *know* what I mean."

"Look Kevin, I'm really very flattered that you like me. You're a very nice guy. But save your breath. There just ain't no way we'll ever see each other any place but right here." The record ends and the cowbell rings. He hands her his last ticket and they start to dance again.

"You probably won't believe this, but my friends brought me here to...well...you know what I mean."

194

"Yeah, I guess I do."

"Look Suzanne, give me your number. I'll memorize it. I'll take you to dinner. You won't have to *do* anything. Just have dinner with me. OK?"

"Kevin…I want you to look at me. I mean *really* look at me."

"What do you think I've been doing all this time?"

"Just tell me: do you think you could ever trust me, knowing what I do for a living? Do you know how I feel about myself? Do your really know *any*thing?"

"Don't feel bad. People can change. You're young! And you're beautiful."

"OK, I'll make a deal with you."

"You're on!"

"Maybe you won't like the deal."

"What've I got to lose?"

"Look, give me your number. Just say it. I've got a great memory."

"Will you call me?"

"No promises. But maybe I will."

He tells her his number and she repeats it. The record ends. Then the cowbell rings. There are tears in his eyes and he waves goodbye. But she has already turned away. As he walks toward the men's room, another guy asks her to dance.

Mike and Vinnie are waiting for him. "Ready to leave?" asks Mike.

"Yeah, let's go."

On the way out, Kevin manages to avoid looking at the dance floor. When they get outside the hot air hits him like a furnace.

"Kev, are you alright?" asks Vinnie.

"I don't know if I should be happy or depressed."

"Hey, we saw what happened in there. Don't worry. Yuh can get yuh rocks off the next time."

"Mike, you don't *get* it do you?"

"Get *what*?"

"Oh, forget it. It doesn't matter."

195

2

Weeks went by, but she didn't call. Kevin knew by now that she never would. So one Saturday evening, without saying anything to Mike or Vinnie, he made another trip into the City and walked up the stairs to Humpers' Heaven. He entered the dance hall, bought some tickets, and looked around. She wasn't there.

He asked another woman to dance. "Is Suzanne here tonight?"

"Suzanne? I don't know no Suzanne."

"Tall, light brown hair, blue eyes. Really beautiful."

"Sounds like you're stuck on her. Oh, wait a minute! I think you mean Kathy. You see, we never use our real names. Yeah, Kathy. No, she don't work here no more."

Kevin thanked her, handed her the rest of his tickets, and went home. On Monday morning he enlisted in the Marines.

When he informed his parents that he had enlisted, his mother cried and his father organized a huge going away party at the Veterans of Foreign Wars hall in their neighborhood. Besides his friends and family, there were dozens of older guys, most of them with big beer bellies, and florid complexions. They all wore what were called "overseas caps." Most of them happily told old war stories about the action they saw in "the Big One." He was miserable.

3

His mother had wanted him to go to college and his father had wanted him to follow him into the police force. He had actually enrolled in the evening program at Brooklyn College and was taking a couple of courses. In fact, the day after finals, he would be leaving for boot camp.

He really needed a change of scenery, and he was hoping, once and for all, to forget about Kathy. Mike and Vinnie never said anything, but he knew that to them she was just another whore. Well, they were right about one thing: he was still a virgin. But come to think of it, they were too. All talk and no action.

The Marines was no piece of cake, but two years later, Kevin was a free man. And *man* was he free. The sixties were almost in full swing. Soon he was "getting laid left and right" and whatever was left of his lingering gloom had gradually vanished. Still, he was never completely happy. He still thought about Kathy, and somehow none of the women he met could ever measure up. He knew this was unfair. He remembered one really lovely woman who cried when they broke up. Her words would haunt him for years: "You never gave me a chance!"

And she was right. How could she compete with a fantasy?

Every so often he thought he saw her. But he was always mistaken. His friends told him he was just using Kathy as an excuse for never getting involved. Still, he never completely gave up hope of someday finding her. He even went back again to Humpers' Heaven. But the building had been torn down, replaced by a twenty story apartment house.

It turned out that the two years he spent in the Marines enabled him not just to go to college, but even to pick up a Master's degree in political science, all under the G.I. Bill. When he got a full-time teaching job at St. Francis College in Brooklyn Heights, he decided to continue on in the PhD program at NYU.

Life was good. Most guys would kill for the social life he was leading. He had more women than he knew what to do with, and there were parties every weekend if he wanted to meet still more. But there was still a huge void in his life, and there was nothing he could do about it.

4
February 4, 1972

It would be Kevin's first bar mitzvah. He and Jake were friends from *St Francis*, but rarely socialized outside the college. After he thanked Jake for the invitation he asked if there was anything he needed to know in advance.

"Just pretend you're going to a confirmation."

"That's *it?*"

"Here's the deal: There's a short service—in English—and the kid reads from the Torah. *That* part's in Hebrew. Then we party.

"So I dress for a party?"

"Look, Kevin, this may be the seventies, but no body shirts and bell bottoms. Wear a business suit."

"I guess I can do that. Will there be any hot women there?"

"Is *that* all you're interested in?"

"Is there anything else?"

"Kevin, I'm surprised at you. Not only are you a respected faculty member at St. Francis, but you have such a fine parochial school background. I heard Saint AUGustine, was quite the place."

"Actually, it's pronounced Saint AugUSTine: the accent is on the second syllable. But that was then and this is now. Hey Jake, what about *you?* You teach here too."

"I'm just one of the token Jews. Besides, I teach accounting, and you have to be Jewish to teach that subject."

"Touche."

"Or as the members of the tribe say, *Tushie.*"

"Doesn't that mean something like 'ass.'"

"In Yiddish, yes. In French, I think it has something to do with fencing."

"OK, back to the bar mitzvah: will all the women be as beautiful as Ruthie?"

"*No* one is as beautiful as Ruthie. But I promise you, there will be one or two good-lookers."

"I really like the way you're still in love with your wife after all these years."

"What's not to love?"

5
April 22, 1972

Kevin walked into the synagogue, was handed a prayer book and a yarmulke (skull cap), and took a seat near the back.

He noticed that the men and women were not segregated, as he had thought they would be. *Well, this makes things a lot easier.* But he was sitting too far back to get a good look at many of the women, so in the meanwhile, he just listened to the service.

Jake had promised that the service would be short. Before he knew it, Joey had whizzed through his Haftorah (Torah reading) and they all went downstairs to the catering hall.

After finding his table, Kevin finally got a chance to look around and scope out the interesting women. *But probably the best ones would be married.* So he headed over to Jake and Ruthie's table, congratulated Joey, discretely handed him an envelope, and then chatted with the proud mother.

"Ruthie, it is so nice to once again see the most beautiful woman in the world."

"Kevin! Flattery will get you everywhere. So how are all the brothers doing?"

"You know the deal. Jake and I are not family to them, and probably me more than Jake. You must have some idea how it is in first generation Irish families, with so many girls becoming nuns and boys becoming priests. At least they can't have it in for Jake somehow failing them."

"Well, a job's a job. Maybe someday the brothers will have a more liberal attitude."

"Oh, they already have."

Ruthie lifted an eyebrow. "Do tell." She knew all about Kevin's wicked sense of humor.

"True story. You know that the Franciscans are an old Irish order, which is a bit strange considering that St. Francis lived in Italy. So I was talking last week to Brother Michael, and I asked him when the brothers would finally become integrated. Well Michael gives me this big smile and says, 'The brothers already *are* integrated. Just last year we took in an EYE-talian."

"Kevin, you are too much. Look, I want you to have a good time. If you are interested in any of the young women here, just tell us. Jake and I know which ones are 'eligible.'"

Half way through the dinner he saw her. How could he have missed her? That long light brown hair and those blue eyes. And that sad smile.

Then he knew he must be mistaken. It had happened before. Even though a few women had *looked* the same, as soon as they opened their mouths, he was instantly let down.

He had to get a hold of himself. Kevin, the big ladies' man, still carrying a torch for so many years. Well, everyone has a weak spot, and that was his.

"Are you al*right?*" Kevin looked up. An older woman seated across from him looked very worried.

Kevin thanked her for her concern. "Did you ever see someone you thought you knew from a long time ago?"

"Sure, and then it turns out they're someone else. So that just happened to you?"

"Yeah, you see that woman over there? I thought I once knew her when I was a kid."

"Well, we all change. But who knows? Maybe you should talk to her. You know, the band is getting ready to play. Why don't you ask her to dance?"

He thanked her, stood up, and slowly walked over to the woman. She didn't notice him until he was a few feet away.

"Excuse me, would you like to dance?"

"Thank you. But I'm not much of a dancer."

"Neither am I. Would it be alright if I sat down?"

"Of course."

"Are you part of the family?"

"I suppose you could say that."

"I work with Jake. So he and Ruthie are the only ones I know here."

"Do I *know* you?

"In what sense?"

She smiles. "I suppose we can eliminate the biblical sense."

"Suppose?"

"Well, if *you* won't tell, then *I* won't tell."

"A nice boy never tells."

"*Are* you nice?"

200

Now he smiles. "I'm so nice, I would probably bore you to death."

"Correct me if I'm wrong, but I am beginning to get the impression that you are offering up this line of bullshit?"

"Blame it on heredity. I come from a long line of bullshitters. I'm Irish."

"Oh yeah? More than *I* am?" she says.

"More Irish or more of a bullshit artist?"

"Take your pick."

"May I ask you a personal question?"

"That depends," she replies.

"On what?"

"On what you ask me, silly."

"OK, what are two Micks doing at a bar mitzvah?"

"I got special permission from the Pope to attend," she said.

"I didn't need his permission. I'm here on official business." He took out his wallet and showed her a card with his photo.

"St. Francis College?"

"Yes. I'm a brother."

"You're a *Franciscan* brother? Hey, are you pulling my leg?"

"Given my vocation, wouldn't that be inappropriate? Remember, I've taken a vow of celibacy, And you, my child. I am sure that you are as pure as the driven snow."

"Don't bet on it."

"Well I'm sorry, but I won't be able to help you. Although occasionally I *have* pinch hit for Father O'Malley."

"The next time I go to confession, I'll ask for you."

"So tell me, what did you say your name was?"

"I didn't."

"Excuse me m'am. May I ask your name?"

"I thought you'd never ask. You may call me Mrs. Robert Schwartz."

"*Really*! Brother Kevin and Mrs. Robert Schwartz. We'd make quite a couple."

"Hey, there were worse matches," she said.

"Yeah, and some of them ended up getting burned at the stake."

"You might even say—are you ready for this, Brother Kevin? —they were 'well done.'"

"What a groaner!"

"I can only work with the material that's available."

"So I gather, then, that you're not."

"I'm not what?" she asked.

"Not available."

"What about *you*? You're even *less* available."

"Well, if you're willing to break a vow, maybe I can break one too." he replied.

"You're *serious*?"

"Find out."

6
April 24, 1972

A few minutes after Jake got into work on Monday, Kevin stopped by his office.

"Jake, thanks so much for inviting me. I had a great time."

"And thank *you* so much for giving Joey that very generous check."

"No problem. We get paid very handsomely."

"Right! I don't know what I'd do if I didn't still have my accounting practice."

"How about lunch today?"

"OK, Kevin. I'll pick you up at your office at noon. You want to eat out or in?"

"We can go across the street."

"Great! See you at 12."

7

After they ordered, Jake looked at Kevin and smiled. So, tell me already, what's on your mind?"

"It's that obvious?"

"Spit it out!"

"I met a woman at Joey's bar mitzvah."

202

"*Mazel tov!* Oh, in case you don't know, that means "Good luck!"

"Jake, my Yiddish is almost as good as yours."

"So who's the lucky woman?"

"She told me her name is 'Mrs. Robert Schwartz.'"

"Kathy?"

"Is *that* her name?"

"So she told you her name was 'Mrs. Robert Schwartz?'"

"What's the deal?"

"Do you like her?"

"I think a lot."

"I've heard *that* before."

"Al*right* already! Enough with the third degree. What's the story with her?"

"OK, let me begin at the beginning. My cousin, Robert, is a complete prick."

"Nobody's perfect."

"Yeah, but some people are less perfect than others. Robert, who I haven't seen in a couple of years, is… how can I put this? He's a lying crook."

"Are you trying to say that you don't like him?"

"Like? *Like?* I hate the bastard, and so does everyone else in the family. He has borrowed, swindled, embezzled, and outright stolen hundreds of thousands of dollars from his parents, his sisters, and from some of his aunts, uncles, and cousins."

"Why did everyone put up with him?"

"Well, he can be very charming, very persuasive."

"What about Kathy? Why did she marry him?"

"Kathy's a special case. Her father disappeared when she was maybe thirteen or fourteen. She had a couple of younger brothers and a younger sister. Their mother struggled to support the family, but then she got breast cancer and Kathy had to drop out of high school and go to work. They had no medical insurance, and remember—that was years before Medicare and Medicaid. We don't know what happened during that period, because Kathy won't talk about it. She says it's just too depressing. "

"Wow! That had to be just awful."

"When she met Robert, she must have been in her mid-twenties. Her mother had just died and she was really depressed. He seemed like a knight in shining armor. And he was a complete con man. So finally, there was someone to rescue her."

"*Did* he?"

"For a while it seemed that way. And everyone in the family loved her, despite the fact that she was a *shiksa*—a woman who is not Jewish."

"*Shiksa* I know."

"Anyway, a couple of years ago he just disappeared. But before he did, he did perform one *mitzvah* (good deed). Kathy had had him served with divorce papers, and he signed them just before he took off."

"What's funny is that she told me her name is "Mrs. Robert Schwartz.""

"Yeah, she does that a lot."

"Why?"

"She likes to remind herself of finally being free of the bastard."

"Jake, have you and Ruthie talked to Kathy since the bar mitzvah?"

"What do *you* think?"

"I have a sneaky suspicion that you have."

"She didn't happen to ask you guys any unusual questions did she?"

"I'll give you two guesses."

"Yes and yes."

"I'm afraid she did have just one question about you, Brother Kevin."

8

She was expecting his call. "Brother Kevin!"

"Mrs. Robert Schwartz!"

204

"Is this about official church business or is this a social call?"

"Actually, it's about both."

"And how may I help you?"

"Well, I'm afraid this is of a somewhat personal nature and would best be discussed in person. But only if you can fit me into your busy schedule."

"Let me check my calendar... Ah, I just had a cancellation and can fit you in at seven tomorrow evening."

"Outstanding! I will try not to take up too much of your time. Let me just jot down your address and we'll be all set."

9

As he turned the corner and began to walk down her block, he whistled a song he remembered from *My Fair Lady*, which was called, "The Street Where You Live." He could not believe that after all this time, he might finally have found her. And in his head, he heard a little voice that kept repeating, "Just take it slow... Take it slow...Take it slow."

She lived in a brownstone. He rang the bell and then he heard her footsteps. She opened the door and he just stood there looking at her. He felt exactly like he had felt when he saw her for the first time.

"Well, Brother Kevin, are you going to just stand there, or would you like to come in?"

"Oh, sorry... yes... yes I would like to come in."

They stepped into her living room. "First, I owe you an apology," he said. "I want you to take another look at this." And he took out his wallet and handed her his St. Francis ID.

"You showed me this at the Bar Mitzvah."

"Yeah, but take a close look at it."

"It has your photo, your name, and it says "Faculty.""

"Right. But you'll notice that it says nothing about being a Franciscan brother."

"You mean you're *not* really a Franciscan brother after all?"

"No, and I didn't want to start off by telling you a lie."

"Then why *did* you?"

205

"Kathy, it's a really long story."

"And it's not a bullshit story?"

"No more than the one I heard the other day from a Mrs. Robert Schwartz."

"Touche."

"Or tushie, as we say in Yiddish."

"I think you've been hanging too much with Jake."

They were sitting next to each other on the couch. He reached over very, very tentatively and stroked her cheek. She leaned in toward him and he very lightly touched her lips with his finger tips. They began to kiss, and when he felt her tongue, he knew what was next and what came after that.

He heard the voice again, "Just take it slow…" as he began sucking on one of her fingers. This would be the first time in his life he ever made love. And he prayed that it was Kathy's first time too.

10

The next words he heard were, "Not bad for a Franciscan brother."

"You're a virgin until you've made love to one of the brothers."

"Is that a fact?"

"Well, I hate to tell you, but we're just getting warmed up."

"Oh yeah? Can you prove it?"

"Well, it happens to be a very long and complicated theological proof."

"I've got all the time in the world."

Hours later, as they lay there holding each other, he told her that he had another confession to make.

"Two confessions in one night? You've been a very bad boy."

"Let me begin by telling you that since just after my 18th birthday, I have been in love with just one woman."

"Kevin, you're making me jealous."

"Now that's the really weird thing. I want to be very clear about this. I'm not bullshitting you. It's the gospel truth."

206

"Yes Brother Kevin." And then she starting tickling him.

"I am *not* ticklish!"

"No? So why are you laughing?"

"Just to make you feel good."

"OK, try to stop."

"Not till you stop tickling me."

"Fine, I'll stop."

"Good. I said that I've been carrying a torch for a woman since I was eighteen."

"Right! So what's so weird about that?"

"Well, Kathy, I'm going to tell you something that's even weirder."

"Wait! I think I know. You're actually the Pope."

"Be serious!"

"I *am* being serious…Look, this is my serious face…See how serious I am?"

"I can't see your face in the dark."

She takes his fingers in her hand and guides them up to her face. Soon they're making loving again.

11

They wake to the sound of the alarm. Before he even opened his eyes, he felt her in his arms. She reached over and turned off the alarm, and then snuggled back again.

"Five minutes—and then I've got to get dressed for work."

"And I've got all the time in the world. I'm off today."

"Well, I don't have such a cushy job."

"Can we see each other tonight?"

"*What!* You want to do this *again?*"

"Sure, why not?"

"OK, then. Since you put it so elegantly."

12

That evening she came to *his* place. Kevin also lived in a brownstone. Right behind the Hotel St. George, it was in the north end of Brooklyn Heights. She looked around his apartment, commented on his photographs, and then she said, "I hope that this time at least you'll feed me."

"You don't smell anything?"

"Is that meatloaf?"

"It sure is. Please sit. Dinner will be served in thirty seconds."

"Meatloaf and a salad. And wine."

"Were you expecting the traditional Irish seven-course meal?"

"A potato and a six-pack?"

He smiled. "Are you ready for confession?"

"Let's save it for dessert."

"Kathy, I need to tell you something now."

"Shoot!"

"I can't eat with one hand."

"Oh, OK. You can have your hand back until we finish eating."

13

"Are you ready to take confession?"

"Yes, my son."

"And no tickling this time."

"Of course not. I know you're not even ticklish."

"All right. You better be sitting down for this."

"I *am* sitting down."

"Let's go into the living room."

"OK."

"Kathy, this is all going to sound crazy. But please hear me out."

"Sure."

"Promise?"

"I promise."

"Can you remember that when we met at the bar mitzvah, you asked me if you knew me?"

"Yes. Actually I do. You looked like someone I must have known a long time ago. But I was probably wrong."

"So you really don't remember me from a long time ago?"

"*Should* I?"

"Last night, when I told you that I was carrying a torch for a woman I met when I was 18? Well, that's true."

"So you're telling me that you've been in love all this time with someone else?"

"Are you ready for this?"

"Ready for *what*?"

"I've been in love with someone for eleven years, eight months, and twenty-six days."

"You kept track?"

"Not exactly. Let me ask you a really bizarre question. Can remember where you were on the evening of August 1, 1960?"

"Off hand, no."

"If I tell you right now, I want you to promise me that you won't freak out."

"Let me think about this for a minute. You said that you have been in love with a woman since August 1, 1960. And you're asking me where I was on that date. Are you asking me what I *think* you're asking me?"

He didn't answer. And then she saw this strange look on his face. He slapped himself on the forehead and started to smile.

"No! *Wait*! I just realized something! Kathy! This is amazing! I can't believe what's just happened!"

"*What?*"

"Forget everything I've been telling you. Forget about the confession. I'm an *idiot*!"

"Keep going. I'm beginning to like this."

"Let me put it *this* way. Did you once see me somewhere? It doesn't matter. Did I actually see you eleven years ago? *That* doesn't matter either. I just this minute realized that *none* of it matters!"

"And why is that?"

Let me show you.

14

209

They woke up the next morning in each other's arms. And that's how they fell asleep the next night. And the night after that.

Did she ever ask again who he thought she was? And did he ever tell her? It doesn't matter.

THE PROGNOSIS

1

When we're dying, we can't pack a suitcase. As they say, "You can't take it with you."

Let's consider a somewhat less drastic decision. If you had to give up every person or thing in your life but one, what or who would that be? For me, the answer to that question was a no-brainer.

2

When we got home from the doctor's office, Robert needed to lie down for a while. I made some tea, but Robert didn't want any. I sat at the edge of the bed, and reflexively placed his hand on his forehead.

"You know, Craig, you don't get a fever just from visiting the doctor."

I smiled. "Well, I'm certainly glad to see that you haven't lost your sense of humor."

"No, not at all! They say you keep it right up to the end."

"Please, Robert. Spare me the melodramatics."

"*Fine!*"

"Can we have a serious conversation?"

"So talk!"

"You heard what the doctor said. If the lump is malignant, she'll operate, and then she'll do more tests. That's not exactly a death sentence."

"No, but then, in a couple of weeks, we'll be back in her office, and she'll tell us a few cells were found in my lymph nodes. And then..."

"Yeah, I know. You'll need chemo and radiation."

I waited, but Robert didn't reply. He had a far-off look. Finally, he rolled over to one side to face me more directly. "I don't think I can go through that again."

"Are you saying that that wasn't as much fun for you as it was for *me*?"

This got a smile.

"I know I'm over-reacting. Maybe they can just cut out the tumor and that will be the end of it. But this time I'm expecting the worst."

"No, the worst—the absolute worst, was the third time."

"Agreed. But in retrospect, had I known how awful the treatment would be, I think I would have chosen to die instead."

"Maybe. But that was before they prescribed medical marijuana."

That got a chuckle out of him.

"Seriously, Robert—and I *am* being selfish about this..."

"Yeah, I know, you never want to lose me."

"Well, I'm glad to hear that even *you* listen some of the time."

Robert didn't answer. When I noticed his regular breathing, I got up, tiptoed out of the room, and shut the door.

3

An hour later, I found myself lying on a couch in the living room, a book on my chest. It had grown dark outside, and I could hear the rush hour traffic.

I thought about how Robert and I had met at a ridiculous dinner party in Brooklyn Heights. I could not remember who invited me, but after a few glasses of wine, it felt like we all had become great friends. We decided to drive across the bridge into Manhattan. There was a piano bar on Grove Street in the Village. It was called *The Five Oaks*.

Anyone could go in there and sing his heart out. No matter how good or bad you were, everyone generously applauded. You could walk in alone, with another guy, or maybe with a whole party of friendly people, and you would quickly feel right at home.

Robert was with someone else, but he and I had been eying each other all evening. When his date went to the bathroom, he slipped me his phone number. As I took it, I squeezed his hand and he blew me a kiss.

That was thirty-seven years ago. Who knows? We might have saved each other lives. We had met just when AIDS was beginning to reach epidemic proportions. We lost dozens of friends, but like other monogamous couples, we were spared.

We had our fights, but who didn't? Since the early nineties, we've been living in Chelsea, where the you-know-who have practically taken over. I guess you know that's happened when no one notices you strolling around the neighborhood.

I wondered if Robert intuited something—something that even the doctor couldn't know. Maybe this time he would not be able to dodge the bullet. Perhaps he was just tired of trying.

I tried to picture life without him. Would I expect him to be there when I got home? Would I imagine crawling into bed with him—and waking up in the morning expecting to see his face?

Just then, I heard the toilet flush, and then Robert's feet padding down the hall. He looked a lot better. He was even smiling.

4

A week later his doctor operated. After she finished, and Robert's chest was stitched up, she asked me to join them in the recovery room. She explained that because he was coming out of sedation, he might not remember everything she said.

The entire tumor did not need to be removed—just the malignant part. So, while Robert lay on the operating table, slices of tissue were sent to the hospital's pathology lab. That's why the operation took almost four hours.

While she was confident that they had removed everything, the lymph node test would be crucial. If no cancer cells were found, we would be home free.

5

A few weeks later, it was time for the test. That morning, I had a revelation. Did it really matter how the test came out? Would Robert get a new lease on life, or perhaps a conditional death sentence? Would we be able to go back to how things were, or would we see our life together coming to an end?

It was just then that I realized an important truth. You know those "crazy people" holding signs proclaiming, "The end is coming"? Well, they've got *that* right!

One day, the end *will* come. But in the here and now, while we still have each other, we have everything that life could offer.

THE ROMANTIC

1

I'd like to tell you about my dear friend, Nancy. But before we go any further, let me put all my cards on the table. I am a very nonjudgmental person. I am also what used to be called a metrosexual. That is a heterosexual man living in a large city—a man who is extremely well groomed and loves to shop for very fashionable clothing. Today the term, metrosexual is kind of dated, but then again, so am I. But let me assure you that while I might *look* a little gay, I *do* like the ladies.

Why am I telling you all this? Just to let you know that I would never say anything bad about my friend. Of course, I *can*, on occasion, be just a tad caddy. But Nancy knows that I would never tell a soul about her indiscretions. So, it goes without saying that what I'm going to tell you about my dear friend must be held in the strictest of confidences.

2

Nancy has always had a thing for younger men. While quite attractive, she *does* have a few liabilities. Let's start with her very short-lived work life.

Her first full time position was with a travel agency. Many dozens of times a day Nancy had to answer the phone with a cheery, "Travel with Trudy. How may I help you?"

Nancy hated her job, and more than anything about it, she hated Trudy. Almost every day, she would complain to me about "that dried up old piece of shit."

"So you don't like her?"

"*Like*? What's there to *like*? She screams at everybody in the office all day long, but when she's on the phone with a client, she's so sugary sweet, she makes me want to puke."

After less than a month on the job, she quit. "What reason did you give?"

"What *reason*? *I'll* give you a reason! I'll give you a *thousand* reasons!"

"Yeah, so I'm waiting."

"Just last Friday, she wouldn't let me leave an hour early, so I could get ready for a date."

"OK."

"Don't you *get* it, Franklin? The bitch was jealous of me!"

I waited for a further explanation, but I guess she figured that it was all quite clear how Trudy's obsessive jealousy gave Nancy no choice but to quit.

3

Nancy's next job was as an "editor" for a group of soft porn magazines. The office was surprisingly sedate, considering the subject matter that it produced. Most of the men were middle-aged, and none was what she considered "marriage material."

The only other women were two older ladies, both of whom were amazingly fast typists. Nancy had never learned to type, but luckily her job was mainly copy editing. She wondered what she would say if she were asked to model. And what would her *parents* say if they ever found out? She had told them she was working for a company that published religious magazines.

The managing editor actually *liked* her. The only problem was that she had been hired for a nine-to-five job, albeit with a little flexibility. Still, her one or two pm arrival times called for

216

just a bit too *much* flexibility. But along with her dismissal notice, she was given a glowing recommendation.

<h2 style="text-align:center">4</h2>

Her next and last position was with Braniff Airlines. They had created quite a stir with their TV ads, which included celebrities like New York Jets quarterback, Joe Namath, who was shown wearing a fur coat. In each ad, the celebrities would proclaim, "If you've *got* it, *flaunt* it!"

After working in reservations for just a couple of months, Nancy received the news that the company had gone bankrupt. She swore to me that she was not the cause. But it was the last job she ever held.

Nancy might have been called a college dropout, but that would greatly overstate her academic record. She had managed to drop out of four different colleges, while somehow accumulating a grand total of just three credits. And those, she conceded, were evidently due to a clerical error.

Nancy's parents were amazingly tolerant people, at least when it came to their only child. Their greatest wish was that someday Nancy would find a man who was actually good enough for her. So it was not surprising that they kept cheering her on as she bounced from one failed relationship to the next.

The first of these that I can remember was her involvement with a dentist—a man who happened to be several years younger than she was. Just out of dental school, Norman had an office only a few blocks from Nancy's apartment. Although she was thirty-two years old, she still lived at home.

Norman's office was located on Yellowstone Boulevard, one of the main thoroughfares of Forest Hills, a nice middle class neighborhood in the heart of Queens. His parents had laid out all the money to set up his office, which they both termed "an investment in his future." He promised to pay them back, but as his mother put it, "Norman, it's the *least* we can do for you!"

Norman wasn't the most handsome young man in Forest Hills, but everyone agreed that he was a nice guy. OK, maybe he was a little overweight, and he did have that stupid laugh, but those were just superficialities that could be overlooked.

One morning, when Nancy woke up with a really awful toothache, she rushed over to Norman's office. The receptionist, who was vigorously chewing gum, listened to Nancy's plea and then informed her that she could not see Dr. Gutfriend without an appointment. Nancy told her that she was in tremendous pain and needed to see him immediately.

"Look miss, Dr. Gutfriend is with a patient! I'll have to ask to you leave. Take our card on your way out, and if you call us, we'll see if there are any openings."

"Why can't you do that *now*?"

Just then Dr. Gutfriend peeked into the waiting room. "What seems to be the trouble?"

Before Nancy could answer, she noticed his goofy expression. It was the look of a man who was completely smitten. He excused himself for a minute, ducked into the other room, and asked his patient to please have a seat in the waiting room for a few minutes while he dealt with an emergency.

He proposed to her on their second date. But Nancy decided to play it a little coy. "Norman, we hardly know each other." But Norman persisted, and when he presented her with a ring a week later, she happily accepted.

When I asked her how she really felt about her fiancé, she had a ready answer: "Look, he's a dentist. What's *not* to like?"

5

Nancy's mother was in seventh heaven. Running into friends along Queens Boulevard, she was constantly being congratulated. Maybe there was hope for their *own* daughters. One evening, when Nancy's parents sat together on the living room couch, they had a good laugh over how one of the women had described Norman. What was it she said, exactly? That he was either the *pick* of the season or the *catch* of the season.

218

"So, what is he," asked Nancy's father, "a piece of fruit or a fish?"

But as luck would have it, Norman's parents were less than thrilled with their son's choice of bride. Surely, he could have done a lot better. Maybe he wasn't the brightest candle in the menorah, but Norman was certainly a *good* boy. *And* he was a dentist! But that *woman*, that *fortune hunter*! What did their son *see* in her?

And then came the migraines. At first Mrs. Gutfriend played the martyr. "They're nothing. I'll get over them soon." But they kept getting worse. Nancy was sure Norman's mother was faking it, but she pretended to be sympathetic. After all, this unpleasant old lady was practically family.

The day that Nancy and Norman found a wedding hall, the migraines grew even worse. Mrs. Gutfriend refused to even get out of bed. Well, it wasn't hard to see where all this was going. And predictably, the day the wedding was called off, the migraines miraculously disappeared.

6

When Norman asked her to please see him one last time, she was pretty sure he would ask her to return the ring. They met at a Cantonese restaurant about three miles down Queens Boulevard, where they would be sure not to run into anyone they knew. It turned out that he had much more important things on his mind than the ring.

First, he said, he wanted to apologize for having caused her so much anguish and embarrassment. She waited, knowing there would be a lot more he wanted to get off his chest.

The second thing he told her was a real shocker. You might as well know that I don't consider myself a *real* dentist. When I couldn't get into any American dental schools, my father made a large contribution to a real fly-by-night dental school in the Caribbean. *That's* how I got my degree."

When she started to say something, he held up his hand like a stop sign, so she knew he had still more to say.

"My parents spent over a hundred thousand dollars to set me up in that office. And when I announced our engagement, they threatened to make me pay back all the money they had spent on me. They said that if I married you, all that money was just going down the drain."

He stopped talking. She waited, but after a minute or so, she realized that he had finished. She stood up and walked out of the restaurant. As she walked along Queens Boulevard, she began feeling better and better. Before she was even halfway home, she was in a great mood.

When Nancy filled me in on that last supper with Norman, I felt that the broken engagement was the best thing that ever happened to her. And somehow, it reinforced my suspicion that deep down, she was truly a romantic. In fact, just a year later, she would meet the man who she would always call "the love of my life."

7

They met in an elevator in an Upper Eastside luxury building when she was on the way to a party. He was tall, thin, had pale blue eyes, and a lovely smile. The second she laid eyes on him, she knew that *he* was the one. Indeed, it didn't bother her in the least that he was in uniform. She whispered into his ear, "When do you get off work?"

She hung around the party till midnight, and then met Brendan in the lobby. He was from Ireland, and his uncle had arranged for this summer job. It was his first time away from home, and the first job he ever had. He was eighteen years old. Nancy, who had just turned thirty-three, confessed to being twenty-four.

Since neither of them had a place where they could go, they decided to just have coffee. He was staying in the Bronx with his uncle's family, and Nancy of course, still lived with her parents. And anyway, Brendan would be returning home in just a few days.

He walked her to the subway and as they stood near the turnstiles, they kissed. Nancy later told me that she actually felt a jolt run through her. She knew then that if she didn't see him again, she would regret it for the rest of her life.

So, she asked him for his address in Ireland. While he was writing, he asked if she had ever heard of Cork. She hadn't. Well, my dad has always believed in the local blarney—that the women of Cork were the most beautiful women in the world. And if anyone disagreed, he pointed at my mum, as if that settled the argument.

Nancy promised him that she'd write, and they waved goodbye.

In her first letter, she asked him if he liked surprises. He said he did. She arrived in Cork two days later.

After checking into a hotel, she dialed Brendan's number. He was amazed to hear her voice. "Gee Nancy, this call must be costing you a fortune!"

"Actually, it's a local call."

"What are you talking about?"

"Would you believe I'm in Cork? You did say you liked surprises."

8

The next day, Brendan's father decided it was time for a long overdue "talk" with his son. It was the talk that perhaps hundreds of generations of fathers and sons had shared. But *this* one would be a bit more complicated, thanks to that strange woman who had arrived in town. So first he enumerated all the reasons why his son should not get involved with her.

Brendan seem noncommittal. He just nodded from time to time, without saying much of anything. Finally, his dad played his trump card.

"Son, do you realize that you live in the city that has the most beautiful women in the world?"

Brendan smiled. His dad clapped him on the back. "I knew you'd see things *my* way. So I hope you don't mind my asking: What can you possibly see in that old hag?" Brendan didn't say anything, but he was smiling.

"You know, Brendan. I had been meaning to have this chat with you for quite a while, so I'm glad we finally had the chance to have it. Then he reached into his pocket and handed his son a packet of prophylactics. "Do you need any instructions, or do you already know how to use these?"

"I think I'll be able to figure them out. By the way dad, did you ever hear that song, "Girls just wanna have fun?"

"I've heard of it, yes."

"Well, boys, *they* just wanna have fun too."

His father broke into a wide grin. "Alright, lad. Go have some fun!"

9

To this day, Nancy proclaims that her week with Brendan was, by far, the greatest time of her entire life. And the best part was teaching him pretty much everything she knew about sex. But as she did, she knew deep down that she would not be there when he got to apply what he had learned.

Just a year later, he sent her a wedding photo. His bride was quite beautiful. Nancy smiled as she read his note. Kathleen was a local girl—someone he had known since childhood. But then she burst out laughing as she read the post script: We were able to put your wedding present to excellent use!

10

When she was thirty-five, Nancy decided that it was finally time to get her own apartment. So when a share in a small apartment in Greenwich Village became available, her parents agreed to pay the rent until Nancy could find a job. Of course, only a cynic like me would say that the likelihood of *that* happening was no greater than the resurrection of Braniff Airlines.

She and Eileen each had their own room, and they rarely saw each other. An aspiring actress from Wyoming, Eileen was busy going to casting calls and tending bar. And Nancy was busy perusing the personal ads in her search for Mr. Right.

One day she hit pay dirt—figuratively *and* literally. But here's the funny thing. Even though I did meet this guy a few times, I can never remember his name. Let me explain.

If you lived in New York in the late 1970s, you'll remember Son of Sam. That was the nickname of a serial killer who haunted lovers' lanes in search of young women to murder. When he was finally arrested, his face was on TV and in all the papers. He was a dorky looking guy.

Anyway, Nancy's new boyfriend looked like a cross between Ludwig von Beethoven and Son of Sam. I kid you not! Imagine a guy with Beethoven's hair and a really idiotic face.

Only a few years out of law school, he was already a fairly well-to-do corporate attorney. He was twenty-eight. Nancy observed that they were the same age.

From the start, their relationship seemed very promising. Each morning, before he left for work, Beethoven-Son of Sam would leave a few twenty-dollar bills on the night table. And because he was a very fair man, the better the sex, the higher the reward.

Nancy wanted to see if she could get him to leave still more money. So she decided to fake her orgasms. And sure enough, the better she faked, the more twenty-dollar bills she found when she got up. Even Eileen was impressed, and suggested that Nancy had a great future on the stage, albeit in very specialized roles.

But all good things must come to an end. One evening, when Beethoven-Son of Sam came over after work, he asked Nancy to please sit down. There was something he needed to ask her.

Nancy had no idea what could possibly be on his mind. So imagine her shock when he asked her to marry him. She just sat there, completely dumbfounded. Her first thought was—if they *did* get married, would the payments stop?

He must have read her mind, because when he had their marriage contract drawn up, there was a clause guaranteeing that the payments would continue. Still better, she would get an excellent settlement if they divorced.

Nancy's parents were overjoyed at the news. And once the marriage had actually taken place, they readily conceded that Nancy's new husband was indeed quite worthy of their daughter. An added bonus, of course, was that a huge financial burden had finally been lifted from their shoulders.

A week after the wedding, Beethoven-Son of Sam informed Nancy that he had just been transferred to Houston. But there was nothing to worry about, because they could live rent-free in a corporate apartment for up to a year, while they searched for permanent housing.

Initially Nancy was extremely disappointed. But if she didn't like it there, she could always get a divorce.

They moved to Houston a few weeks later and settled into their apartment. Nancy resumed her old routine of sleeping till noon, and then counting up the twenties left on the night table.

And then, there was an unexpected change. Instead of twenties, there were fifties. Well, she thought, don't look a gift horse in the mouth. She wondered if her orgasms could ever be as good for *her* as her screams were for *him*.

Nancy had never learned to cook, since, of course, her mother had done practically everything for her. But they got along fine on the take-out that her husband brought home after work. On the evenings when he had to work late, she just popped leftovers into the microwave.

On afternoons, when it wasn't too hot, Nancy went for long walks. I asked her where she went, and she confessed that she was looking around to see if there were any cute guys.

"So are you saying that Beethoven-Son of Sam is no longer satisfying you?"

"Franklin, 'no longer' is inaccurate. He *never* satisfied me. I guess I just got too used to those piles of twenty-dollar bills. Oh, and by the way, he's now leaving fifties."

One evening, after they had been there for three months, Beethoven-Son of Sam came home and asked Nancy to have a seat. What could it be *this* time?

"Nancy, I hate to do this, but I'm going to have to ask you for a divorce."

"What are you talking about? We just got married."

"Of course, we did. But the thing is, I met someone else."

"Yeah?"

"She's pregnant."

"Holy *shit*!"

"Look, I'm sorry!"

"Sorry doesn't cut it!"

"OK, I know this is kind of crass, but you know the divorce settlement clause in our marriage contract?"

Nancy just nodded, afraid to hear what would come next.

"If you agree to a divorce immediately, I'll increase you alimony payments by fifty percent."

11

Just a few days later Nancy was back in New York. She even managed to hook up again with Eileen, and they found a nicer apartment just a few blocks from where they had been living. And within weeks, she even landed a small part in an off-off-off Broadway play, making certain sounds from off-stage.

She got a few identical gigs, but she never appeared on-stage. It was *then* that she realized that she was on the downhill side of life. Soon she was pushing forty, and then, fifty. One day I asked if she had any regrets.

"Well, you know, Franklin, my life's not quite over yet!"

"So you *still* think you might meet someone?"

"Well, now that you mention it, I've decided to go to Europe."

"Are you hoping to meet a nice young man?"

"Well, the thought *did* cross my mind."

"So where do you plan on going first?" She smiled, but didn't answer.

"England? France? Italy? Maybe Greece?"

"Actually, I was thinking of Ireland."

THERE'S SOMEONE FOR EVERYONE

1

Helene knew for sure that there was *not* someone for everyone. She could even prove it.

Helene does not remember much about her parents. An automobile accident left her orphaned when she was just four years old. What she *does* remember is a sequence of foster homes—some bad, some not so bad—and that she would go through life unwanted and unloved.

And then, one day, she reached the age of eighteen. Suddenly, she was on her own. But in a way, she was still a ward of the state, in this case, the state of Michigan. She had won a full academic scholarship to the University of Michigan.

As it turned out, the school would be her home for the next six years. She was a theater major, and before her junior year, she had a whole new family. In fact, it was the first real family she had ever had. The theater majors were a tight-knit group. Some had been acting since childhood, while others were happy working behind the scenes—mainly designing them.

By the end of her sophomore year, Helene had found herself drawn to Greg, who was a year ahead of her. They were polar opposites. He was a bear of a man, with a bushy beard, long dark hair, and an outgoing personality. He had no pretensions of ever acting, and longed to one day become a great director.

Helene was tall, slim, blonde, and extremely introverted. She could act, but once off-stage she would clam up. One day, Greg walked over to her, knelt before her, and asked her for a date. She burst out laughing.

"Is that a 'yes'?" he asked.

It was. They soon became "an item." When Greg graduated, he decided to stay on at Michigan, so that he could be with Helene. A year later, she joined him in the Theater Department's MFA program.

The department's grad students called themselves the Michigan Mafia, perhaps just for the alliteration. But the name stuck. Years and years later, they still referred to themselves by the initials—the MM. And they laughed when someone overhead them and offered them some M & Ms.

Helene had decided that she was much better suited to working behind the scenes, so she and Greg co-directed a few plays. If you thought there was room for only *one* big ego, you'd be right. But they truly complemented each other.

Greg would supply the cheerleading and the enthusiasm, but also the all-too-public criticism. Helene would quietly put out the fires he started, smooth the ruffled feathers, and give the needed individual help and encouragement. He provided the inspiration; she provided the love.

Together they were a team. Just a minute before one of their plays opened, they would proclaim to the cast: Look out off-off-Broadway, here we *come!*"

There was just one problem: Vietnam. Greg had been able to count on receiving deferments as long as he stayed enrolled as a full-time student. But things did not work out as planned. As the war escalated, his local draft board needed more bodies, and Greg began to smell like fresh meat.

So Helene and Greg went to Plan B. They both were accepted into the Peace Corps. They would soon be teaching their craft to "the natives." They got married at Ann Arbor City

Hall, and invited the entire Michigan Mafia to a dinner at the greasy spoon where they often dined.

2

Just a few months later, after undergoing a rigorous training program, Helene and Greg were sent to Bolivia, along with two assistants—a carpenter and an artist. They settled in a remote village, recruited a local cast, and put on a show. But not in a barn. The show would be staged outdoors.

The main reason they had been sent to Bolivia was probably that the four of them were fluent in Spanish. That was essential. They would be putting on a production of *Fiddler on the Roof* in Spanish.

One might think that the cultural barriers alone would make this enterprise impossible, and indeed, hundreds of Peace Corps projects did not work out as planned. How can you get a cast of South American peasants to empathize with the people in a tiny Jewish *shtetl* in Czarist Russia?

But as they all worked together, Helene and Greg learned just how much in common the people in this village high in the Andes had with their Jewish counterparts—the happy times, the hardships, the celebrations, and the isolation from the outside world. Still, unlike the cast of the Broadway production, not one of these villagers had ever acted before.

Neither Greg nor Helene had ever seen an actual production of *Fiddler on the Roof*. Or even the movie, which actually came out a few weeks after they had arrived in Bolivia. But as they watched their own production begin to come together, Greg suddenly had a great insight.

"Helene, do you realize what this play is?"

She just shook her head "no."

"It's the Jewish *Oklahoma!*"

3

How did all it work out? Helene and Greg will always remember opening night. They had several bedsheets sewn together for the curtain. And behind the curtain, there was a phonograph powered by a generator. To make sure that the fiddler in the opening number could be heard, they managed to partially muffle the noise from the generator.

The show began. A few minutes later, when Helene heard the teenage sisters singing "Match-maker, match-maker, make me a match," she looked at Greg. They both had tears in their eyes. As they peeked out from behind the curtain, they saw that many people in the audience were wiping their eyes. Some were openly crying.

Greg and Helene hugged. They had actually pulled this off! Back in Michigan, they had directed plays that made people laugh. But now they actually made people cry. In fact, they were so happy, they couldn't stop crying.

Years later, when they would tell friends about that moment, the tears would return. It had been the happiest time of their lives.

4

They would remain in Bolivia, and later in Peru, for nearly five years. Toward the end, Helene began to sense that she and Greg were beginning to grow apart. Always a big man, Greg gradually put on more and more weight. She remembered reading somewhere that when someone did that, he was pushing other people away.

Anyway, she knew for sure there couldn't be another woman, because there just *were* no secrets where they were. And while their sex was still good, it slowly became less and less frequent.

They decided that a change of scene might be all they needed, and anyway, their Peace Corps contract was ending. Rather than move back to Ann Arbor, they decided to seek their fortunes in New York.

When they got there, they found a nice three-room apartment that they could afford on the Upper Eastside. In fact, it was so far *up*, it was practically in Spanish Harlem.

They both quickly found jobs teaching English as a second language to Spanish-speakers, and began looking for work in the theater. As the months went by, nothing much changed in their sex life, but Greg began to lose weight. And then he took up running.

They lived just a few blocks from Central Park, and he would get up most mornings at six a.m. to get in a run. Helene was hoping that this new interest in physical fitness was Greg's attempt to make himself more attractive to her.

As things turned out, she was *half* right. One day, as they were having dinner, Greg put down his fork and just stared at her. She knew something was the matter and that it was pretty serious.

"Honey, I just don't know how to tell you this."

"You've met someone else."

He just bowed his head.

They sat there like that, neither one saying anything.

They both knew it was over. Greg packed his things, and by the weekend he had moved out. He gave Helene a phone number and an address, and she knew that it must be *her* apartment.

5

For a few weeks, Helene thought she was dealing with everything pretty well. But she grew more and more depressed. Then she got a call from Harold, an old friend from the MM. He was moving to New York. Could he stay with them a little while, till he found his own place?

Helene did not tell Harold that Greg had left her until he had moved in. Harold quickly realized that Helene was very seriously depressed. She and Greg had been very understanding when Harold had "come out" during his freshman year. As grad students, they often took the younger students under their wing, so to speak.

Within a week of his arrival, Helene stopped working, and began sleeping well into the afternoon. Harold cooked, shopped, and never once mentioned anything about "getting help." He knew, instinctively, that given time, things would work their way out without whatever so-called help "trained professionals" could provide.

It took almost six months. One day, Helene went back to work. A few weeks later, she started going to parties. And before long, she was even dating. In the meanwhile, Harold found an apartment in the building.

The only thing that changed was that, aside from occasionally going to plays, she had lost her passion for the theater. She would never direct again—not even *Fiddler on the Roof.*

6

Helene confided in Harold in a way she never had with anyone else—even Greg. He was a good listener, but what advice could *he* give?

Despite all her progress, he wondered if she would ever get involved with another guy, let alone remarry. Still, if he ever got the chance, he would certainly try to help things along.

But before he could, Helene came to him in a panic. Had he heard that a bunch of the MMs were coming to New York for a couple of days, and there would be a get-together.

"Are you asking me to be your date?"

"Actually, yes. I know Greg will be there with his... his..."

"Roommate?"

"Yes, his *roommate!*"

"Well, then, m'lady, will you do me the honor of accompanying you to this splendid affair?"

7

They had a leisurely late lunch on a weekday afternoon at Sardi's, with a long table all to themselves. Some of the MMs were there with their spouses and significant others. It must have been a little strange to some of the old-timers seeing Greg with another woman, and of course, even stranger seeing Helene and Harold together. The two of them smiled at each other, happy to keep the others guessing. Even Greg would occasionally glance over at them, trying figure out what, if anything, was going on between the two of them.

Perhaps to arouse their curiosity even further, Harold and Helene said their goodbyes, and left before any of the others. As they walked past the window and made their way up Seventh Avenue, they were holding hands.

8

A week later, a letter arrived addressed to Mr. and Mrs. Gregory Miller. It was from some PR hack at the Peace Corps headquarters. Inside was what appeared to be a form letter and a clipping from a newspaper in La Paz, the Bolivian capital. This was the lead: For three weeks every June, a small village in the shadow of the Andes puts on a full-scale production of the famed Broadway play, *Fiddler on the Roof*.

Helene had to stop reading and grab a box of tissues. When Harold got home he took one look at her and just shook his head. She had been doing so well, and now *this*! She had apparently gone through dozens of tissues, and her eyes were red.

"What *happened?*"

"Harold! I know you're not going to believe this, but I've never been happier in my life!"

"If this is you happy…"

"Here, look at this article!"

Harold glanced at it, and then reminded her that he didn't know the lingo.

"Harold. Remember that Greg and I did *Fiddler on the Roof* in Bolivia?"

"Sure."

"Would you believe that the people in that village have continued doing the play?"

"You've gotta be kidding!"

"Scout's honor."

"That is amazing! Does *Greg* know?"

"Not yet. But I'm going to send him this clipping."

233

"But wait! There's more! The director played the oldest daughter when we put it on seven years ago. And next month, she is adding a second play to their repertoire."

"Which one?"

She burst out laughing as she shouted, "*Oklahoma!*"

9

Harold had a theory about Helene. He knew there were tons of great guys out there who would be attracted to her, and that maybe she'd like one of *them*. But having been "abandoned" not just by her parents, but by her husband, Helene could certainly be expected to be gun-shy. And he had a pretty good idea how she would react if it did happen a third time. She would need a guy who could never leave her.

Then, a great opportunity presented itself, but he knew it was a longshot. A guy he knew from the neighborhood had made some not-so-discreet inquiries as to whether Helene was available. And if he could he call her?

Ken was not the best-looking guy in the world, and he was pretty much of a schmuck. He was so neurotic, that it was a miracle he could manage to hold a job. In fact, he was always in trouble at work because he was late half the time. Fortunately, he did not perform any vital services, but he *was* extremely bright, and sometimes quite funny. So, they kept him around.

Once, when Ken and Harold were with a group of friends at a small restaurant, Harold desperately needed to use the men's room, but it was occupied. He told Ken he was going to use the women's room. When Harold returned to our table, Ken stood up, shook his hand, and announced to their dining companions that Harold had "gone where no man had ever gone before."

Harold found Ken very likeable, but he told story after story about his being rejected by women. Even if Helene *did* start dating again, Harold seriously doubted if she would even give Ken a chance. Still, he thought, who am *I* to stand in their way?

With Helene's permission, Harold gave him her number. But Ken never called. As he explained to Harold, he couldn't make the call, because if he asked Helene to go to dinner, she might think he was being chauvinistic by making plans without consulting her. On the other hand, if he left it up to her, then she might think he was a wimp.

"Ken, you *are* a wimp, so what difference would it make?"

"All the difference in the world! Look, *you* know I'm a wimp, and *I* know I'm a wimp. But *she* doesn't! If she got to know me a little better, maybe we could get past that."

Yeah, right, thought Harold. And how are we going to get past that if you won't even pick up the phone to call her?

Harold knew that it would take extraordinary measures to get Ken to make even the first move. There was a party he had been invited to, and he asked Helene if she would like to go. After she agreed, he called the hostess and asked if Ken could come.

"That neurotic schmuck? Are you *nuts?*"

"Not as nuts as *he* is! But if you do me this favor, I will owe you big time."

"Harold, if I didn't love you as much as I do, I'd tell you…"

"To go fuck myself?"

"Exactly."

10

The party was somewhere out in Queens. It was well underway when they got there. Ken had not yet arrived. Harold and Helene had another party to go to, and soon he began to wonder if having Ken invited was such a great idea. Then, just as they were about to leave, Ken arrived. When he saw Helene, he made a beeline for her.

Harold decided they might as well stay awhile, to give Ken a chance to make his move. After half an hour, he pulled Helene aside, and found out that all Ken was doing was making conversation.

"Let me ask you a simple question."

"Shoot!"

"Are you attracted to him?"

"No, but buried somewhere under that pile of neuroses, there lurks a really first-rate mind."

"Oh, he's smart alright. Maybe *too* smart."

"Harold, I don't think anyone can be *too* smart."

"So, you think you might really like him?"

"Yeah, but it's sure hard to tell, because he seems to be hiding under so many layers. And I'm sure you know, Harold, that in some ways, Ken is still a little boy."

"And you find *that* attractive?"

"I do. Especially when that little boy puns in Latin."

"Well, Ken's been pestering me about setting the two of you up."

"*Really?* I never would have guessed it."

Harold got their coats, and when Ken saw them leaving, he rushed over to them.

"Where are you guys going?"

"We have another party."

"Oh."

Suddenly, Harold had a wicked thought. "Helene, where do you live?"

"What kind of a dumb question is that? You live in the same building."

"Humor me."

Helene shot him a look. "I live on East 93rd Street."

"*Really!* Between which Avenues?" asked Ken.

Harold laughed to himself, watching how excited Ken was getting.

"I live between Second and Third."

"I can't *believe* it! I live on East 94th between First and Second!"

"We're neighbors, Ken."

"We *are*! Could I have your number?"

11

As they drove to the next party, Helene asked, "Did I miss something back there?"

"Obviously."

"Care to explain what I missed?"

"OK, Helene. A little background on Ken. I told you he had been pestering me for months for your number."

"Yeah, and I said it was OK if he called me. But he never did."

"That's right. You can see that he's a little disturbed."

"A *little?*"

Harold smiled.

"OK, I'll come clean. I knew there was one thing in the world that excited him about women more than anything else."

"And what might *that* be?"

"Where they live."

"So, why is where I live so exciting? *You* live there. Do *you* find it exciting?"

"No, I don't. It was, of course, exciting to live with you. But no, I didn't find the block *that* exciting."

"So why does Ken?"

"Well, you see, he parks on the street. He's much too cheap to spring for a garage."

"Yes. So where is this going?"

"If you lived on the Westside or downtown, in order to go out on a date with you, Ken would have to give up his parking spot, drive to your neighborhood, and find another parking space. And then, when he went home, he might have to drive around for an hour looking for another spot."

"Oh, I get it, Harold…"

"If he went out with you, he wouldn't have to move his *car!*"

12

Miraculously, just a few months later they got married and Ken moved in with her. Theirs was a match made in heaven. Helene would never worry about Ken ever leaving her. After all, who else would want him?

And Ken? He knew that he would never have to look for another parking space.

THE MOTH AND THE FLAME

Sometimes I like to flatter myself by calling Claudia my ex. My femme fatale. And myself, her old flame.

Sometimes I think of how we danced close, never touching, alone together in a sweating crowd. Aren't *they* a couple! Just look at their eyes.

One night, years into our non-relationship, Claudia told me that she was so drawn to me that it took everything she had to stay away. Which reminded me of a joke. Well, maybe not exactly a joke—a dumb story.

Barry really liked Marsha, but she would never go out with him. When she started going steady, Barry thought that maybe she was doing this just to discourage him from asking her out. So, he persisted even after she was engaged. When her wedding announcements went out, there was further proof.

After the birth of Marsha's second child, Barry could no longer contain himself. He demanded to see her. She agreed, but only if he would never bother her again. When they met, Barry told her of his suspicions about her feelings for him. And how, as she moved toward marriage and motherhood, he had become increasingly convinced that she was doing this only to avoid her true love, Barry. And now that she had gone so far as to have had children, he finally saw the light. His suspicions had vanished. He would never bother her again. She had freed him. And as he left, he said, "Now I can finally get on with my life. Thank you for proving your love to me."

If only my love for Claudia—and hers for me—was that simple. Claudia told me she had stayed away from me, discouraged me, even ignored me for all those years because she knew that if she got too close, I would destroy her.

So, I asked her to marry me. "*Marry* you, Peter? You want me to *marry* you? We've never even gone out on a date."

"And whose fault was *that?*"

"Actually, it was yours. Every time you asked me out I screamed '*Yes!*' Remember how I would smile at you? Remember how I would never say anything?"

"Believe me, I remember. And I wanted you even more. I knew you were trying to be nice to me. To let me down easy. To turn me down without saying no."

"Peter, you are amazing. Didn't you have any idea how much I wanted to just throw my arms around you?"

"So, why didn't you?"

"Peter, you're like a flame."

"Right, and you're a moth."

"Actually, that's a very apt analogy."

"Well, if it is, then how come you haven't gotten burned yet?"

She smiled. "You know, Peter, I think you're really starting to get it. If I were to go out with you even once... No—wait! If I were to touch you, I doubt I would ever be able to stop."

"And your point *is*—?"

"That *is* my point."

"Claudia, work *with* me. You're saying I'm so irresistible that you, the moth, will be burned up by me, the flame?"

"If I get too close."

"Claudia, I *love* you!"

"You may. Although considering the entourage of women that always seems to surround you, I *do* have my doubts."

"*What* entourage?"

"Come now, Peter. Every time I see you, you're talking to some woman. Or two, or three."

"What can I *tell* you? Guys don't like me."

"I can see why."

"Yeah, I guess jealousy can be a powerful thing."

"Seriously, Peter. I *do* think you have problems making commitments."

"Problems? Try my way of life. But believe me: I'd give it up in a second if you'd be with me."

"OK. Let's say, just for the sake of argument that you really could. That would actually make things worse."

"I just lost you."

"We would stay up all night talking. You're a night person and you'd make *me* into a night person. I'd lose my job."

"Just go to sleep. I could stay in another room."

"And I'd know you were there. I wouldn't be able to sleep. I'd come in there to be with you."

"This is getting a little strange. I'm so wonderful that you would literally avoid me. You won't touch me because then you wouldn't be able to stop. Would you say that I'm like a car without brakes?"

"And I'm driving you down a mountain. And the only way to stop is to crash."

"You *could* try throwing it into reverse."

"Think of what that would do to my gears."

"Yeah, Claudia, but it would be a hell of a ride."

"I'm not thinking about the ride. I'm thinking about where I'd end up."

"You'd end up with me."

"Probably not. We'd drive each other crazy."

"Look Claudia, we live only once. At least as far as we know. Hey, wouldn't it be funny if, maybe in some other life, we were together?"

"Right! And I'm sure it was a disaster."

"Don't you believe in free will?"

"I've been exercising my free will."

"Then why don't you exercise your free will by being with me?"

"Peter, we've been over this."

241

"And your answer is—?"

She just smiled. And thinking back, I knew what I should have done. Because I've replayed that moment every day of my life. I reach out very, very slowly and touch her hair. And even more slowly, she reaches up. Her hand is so warm. And she smiles at me.

THE WEDDING DATE

1

Diane is one of my best friends. We hang out, talk on the phone, go out to dinner occasionally, but that's *it*. So, don't go getting any ideas. Yeah, she's very attractive, smart, a lot of fun to be with, but we always been and always *will* be strictly platonic.

When someone asks, "Is there anything going on between the two of you?" Diane might answer, "Not that I know of." My friend, Don, truly believes that if a man and woman are regularly in close proximity, they would inevitably "do it." I actually stayed in Diane's apartment for a couple of nights when my place was being painted. As far as I know, nothing happened.

I'm bringing all this up so that you'll be perfectly clear about our relationship. So, when Diane was invited to a wedding and was asked to come with a date, I was not exactly the first person she thought of. In fact she must have asked five or six different guys who she had either once dated, or maybe was thinking about seeing. But for one reason or another, they all turned her down. So then she asked me. Clearly, she was scraping the bottom of the barrel.

Why *was* this? I happen to be a pretty decent looking guy, but I can well understand why Diane must have been pretty desperate to ask *me* to go with her. First of all, like I already mentioned, Diane and I are buddies. So would *you* want to bring your *brother* to a wedding as your date? And second, let's face it: I *am* quite the ladies' man, if you get my drift. But the third reason why Diane was kind of leery about asking me was the biggie: I *do* sometimes behave inappropriately.

But now it was just one week before the wedding, and Diane just could not bear to show up without a date. She was so desperate that she decided to ask *me*.

"Freddie, how would you like to do me a tremendous favor?"

"Sure. Isn't that what friends are for?"

"Did I ever mention my friend, Amy? Well, she's getting married next Saturday night, and I need someone to go with."

"You know that the Democratic Primary is the following Tuesday, right? I've already committed myself to give my political club all my spare time till then."

"You can't spare *me* a few hours? This is really important to me. I would feel extremely uncomfortable going without a date. I'd stick out like a sore thumb."

"Don't you have anyone *else* to go with?"

"Do you think I'd be asking you if I *did*?"

"Boy, it's *that* bad, eh?"

"Please Freddie, I'm begging you. Do you want me to get down on my hands and knees?"

"Maybe later, but let me tell you what's going on. I'm a volunteer in Bella Abzug's campaign. She's got a great shot at becoming our next mayor, so I really wanted to work on some last-minute stuff over the weekend."

"*Bella Abzug*? How can you even *think* about supporting her? She's abrasive, obnoxious, loud, much too liberal... and I can't stand those big floppy hats she always wears!"

"So are you trying to tell me that you don't *like* her?"

"*Like* her? What's to *like*?"

"Look, I *know* the woman. And while she's all of the things you just mentioned, she's also the most honest, intelligent, and capable candidate in the race. The city is bankrupt, and she's the only one who can bring us out of this mess. And Abe

Beame, who largely got us into bankruptcy, has the *chutzpah* to run for reelection."

"Freddie, I don't care *who* you're supporting for mayor. Look, I'll let you do anything… well, *almost* anything, if you'll come with me to the wedding."

"*Any*thing?"

"I said, *almost* anything."

"OK, then we've got a date!"

"Wait a second! Freddie, what *are* you going to do?"

"Nothing much. Maybe just try to convince a few of the wedding guests to vote for Bella. That's about it."

"Fine. If that's all, I guess I can live with it. Although I'm telling you right up front that *I'm* not going to vote for her."

"It's a deal!"

"Great! So, we're all set?"

"Yes, Diane. I'm looking forward to our date."

"Thanks, Freddie. I really owe you."

2

The next Saturday evening it was still quite light outside when I rang Diane's bell. As soon as she opened the door she blurted out: "Wow! A tuxedo! Freddie, you have done yourself proud."

"Thanks, Diane. You look beautiful. In fact, I'm afraid you'll upstage the bride."

"Oh my! Flattery will get you everywhere. By the way, what's with that stack of papers you've got under your arm?"

"Here, take one. I know you're not voting for Bella, but here's her latest circular. I even had a hand in writing it."

"Freddie? I'm afraid to ask. What are you going to *do* with these? No, don't *tell* me. That way at least I'll have plausible deniability."

"All right! Mums the word. Are we ready to go?"

"I guess so. I don't want to miss the hors d'oeuvres. They're usually much better than the meal."

A few minutes later we arrived at the catering hall. Diane spotted a couple of friends and made all the introductions.

"Diane, where have you been hiding this hunk?"

"Now Karen, Freddie and I are just old friends."

"Yeah, right!"

Diane just smiled. Then I kissed her on the cheek and said, "Darling, I'll be *right* back." As I was leaving, I overheard them talking about me.

"Diane, have *you* been holding out on us? Where did you *meet* this guy? He's gorgeous."

"Elaine, I just told you guys, we're just good friends."

"*Sure* you are."

"*Enough* already! So where are Mike and Joey?"

"Over there by the food tables. You'd think we don't feed them."

A few minutes later, I returned with two large plates of appetizers. I bowed to the three women and said, "Ladies, my name is Freddie. I'll be your waiter tonight. Would you care for some hors d'oeuvres?"

Karen leaned over and whispered to Diane, "He is *so* devoted. I don't know where you got him, but I want one too."

Diane could not believe how well this was going. Maybe she should rethink her relationship with this man. Just then, they were all called into the chapel. Diane took Freddie's arm. She confided that she always cried at weddings, and that she was glad that he was being so nice.

The ceremony was mercifully short, and in less than half an hour they were being ushered into the dining room, while the chapel was being readied for the next wedding party. Diane had managed to use up all their tissues.

"Why do weddings make you so sad?"

"Who said I'm sad?"

Then why are you crying?"

"Because I'm so *happy*. I'm happy for Amy. I'm happy that she finally found someone to love, and... and I'm happy that you've been so nice."

"OK, so when you're happy, you cry. Then I'll know when you're really sad because you'll be laughing?"

This, of course, made her laugh, and she gave me a playful shove." "You know, Freddie, you've made me very happy tonight."

I just stopped and looked at her. Then she took my arm again, and we followed everyone into the dining room.

As we approached our table, we could hear a strange sort of murmuring. And then Diane realized what was causing it. At each place setting on all the tables, there was a picture of Bella Abzug in that damn hat. *Freddie!*

She looked at him and he just smiled at her. "I will *kill* you," she hissed.

"Then I'll die happy. My work here is done."

"I thought we had a *deal!*"

"We do. I'm your date. I'm here for you."

"I think we're having a menage a trois with Bella Abzug— and we're having it in front of all these people."

"I love the imagery. But just like it is between you and me, with Bella and me it's also strictly platonic."

"Very funny!"

"Diane, seriously: I didn't mean to embarrass you."

"Well, you *did!*"

"I don't think anyone actually saw me leafleting the tables."

"Freddie, you walked into the place with a whole stack under your arm. Someone must have seen you and put two and two together."

After we sat down, we introduced ourselves to the other couples at our table. Diane didn't know any of them, but an older woman said to me, "So you like Bella Abzug?"

"Yeah, I think she's great!"

"You were the one who leafleted all the tables?"

"*Bingo!*"

"You must be in politics."

"Yeah, but I hate all the crooks. That's why I'm doing everything I can to get Bella elected."

"That's nice. My son is also in politics. He's a reform Democrat."

"Yeah, me too! I'm in a club on the Upper Westside."

"Really? So is my son. Maybe you know him."

"Well, there are three reform clubs above 59th Street, but you never know."

"I'm very proud of my son. He even knows the mayor. In fact Abe Beame just appointed him Deputy Traffic Commissioner."

This didn't make any sense. If this guy was a reform Democrat, why would Beame—who was a crooked regular Democrat from way back—appoint him to a fairly high job just before the Primary. Even Diane sensed something was wrong. I felt her fingers digging into my arm.

"Are you *sure* your son is a *reform* Democrat?"

"Of course I'm sure. Wait, I'm trying to think of the name of the club he's in. It it's the... the Park something Democrats."

"The Park West Independent Democrats?"

"Yeah, I think that's it."

"I'm not in that club. I'm in the club that's up above 96th Street. But who knows? I might have met him. What's his name?"

"Robert Seinberg."

The words were out of my mouth before the censor in my brain could stop them. "*That* fuck?"

Everyone at the table just stared me. And poor Mrs. Seinberg whispered to her husband, "Oy, oy, oy! Such a thing to say! And at a *wedding*!

Diane was livid. I wanted to crawl under the table and stay there until the wedding was over. There was nothing I could say. Or unsay. I tried to think of how I could apologize. But all I could think of was, "Actually, Mrs. Seinberg, your son is not a *complete* fuck." At least I had the decently to keep my mouth shut.

Somehow, we got through the rest of the wedding. Word quickly spread and everyone at the wedding knew who was responsible for the leafleting. And they would soon hear about "*That* fuck." But the worst of it was that everyone knew what an awful date Diane had brought to the wedding, which was a lot worse than having no date at all.

On the way home, I apologized again and again. Diane admitted that a lot of it was probably her own fault for pressuring me to go to the wedding. And then she asked me to explain what had prompted such an outburst.

"Just around the time that Seinberg got a job in the Beame Administration, we learned that he had evidently been spying on the Abzug campaign, and may have even been sabotaging some of our operations. And to add the icing to the cake, he actually knows virtually nothing about traffic, and probably has a no-show job."

"That's awful! That guy *is* a fuck!"

"Tell that to his mother." She gave me another shove, but then she put her arm around me, which really felt great.

"So, are you going to vote for Bella?"

"Only if she stops wearing those damn hats."

3

Time passes. It's six months later, and sadly, Bella didn't win. Ed Koch, who had started out as a reform Democrat, but was now backed by the political machine bosses, had just been elected mayor, and would take office in a few weeks.

Believe it or not, Diane decided to give me another chance to be her wedding date. I guess some people just never learn. But here's the kicker: Bella will actually be a guest at this wedding. When Diane heard that she would be coming, she said, "For one day at least, can she go without wearing one of those damn hats?" Still, Diane thought it was great that Bella would be there to see us get married.

AT FIRST SIGHT

1

I saw her as soon as I got to the party. She was talking to a couple of guys who seemed to hang on her every word. I had never seen such a beautiful woman. She looked like she could be a ballerina, and with those high cheek bones and soft brown eyes, she could be an actress. I loved the way she smiled, and how she touched one of the guys on the arm.

They looked like Wall Street types, or maybe corporate lawyers, both of them in beautifully tailored suits. It was hard to tell if they were on the same team or just friendly competitors. Never go two on one; you both lose.

There's a great way to meet women at parties, even when they're talking to someone else. You just stand there, a few feet away. Look right *at* them. It doesn't hurt, of course, if you happen to be attractive. I work out, I've got a tan most of the year, and frankly, I'm not too hard on the eyes. I'm not bragging, I'm just stating the facts. And the ladies tell me they just love my sky-blue eyes.

If you stare at a woman long enough, she'll notice. Now the next ten or fifteen seconds will either close the deal—or not. She *will* stare back at you for maybe a second or two, and then, unless she's completely smitten, she'll look away.

Just keep staring. If she looks back again, smile at her. Guaranteed: She'll smile back. Now you can just reel her in.

I waited. Soon she glanced at me, and then turned back to the guys. It took just a few seconds and she looked back at me. I shrugged. *She* shrugged. Then she said something to the guys, and a minute later she joined me.

I whispered to her that those guys were escaped mental patients, and that I was waiting for back-up before taking them to the institution.

She smiled and thanked me. "They really don't look that dangerous."

"No, of course not. But don't let those suits fool you. Those men are very dangerous. But you're safe now."

"*Am* I?" She gave me a big smile and a friendly punch in the arm.

"Do you *want* to be?"

"I guess it depends on whom I'm with."

"Well, in the meanwhile, may I ask you a personal question?"

"Shoot!"

"Do you think our children will have blue eyes or brown eyes?"

"Aren't we getting a little ahead of ourselves?"

"Sorry, my name's Brad."

She shook hands. "Gwen."

"Nice to meet you, Gwen. Here's my card."

"You're a *theatrical* agent?"

"Oops! Wrong card."

"Why do you *have that* card?"

"Are you an actress?"

"No, but I do get that question a lot."

"You're amazingly beautiful."

"Thank you! You're not so bad-looking yourself."

"Well thank you! Do you have a card?"

She reached into her bag and gave me a card.

"Gwen Hardy, M.D. I'm impressed!"

"So, if you're not a theatrical agent, what do you actually do?"

I handed her another card.

"Bradley Gilmore, CPA. *I'm* impressed!"

"Not as much as *I* am. So do you date accountants?"

"All the time!"

"So would you consider going out with me?"

"Sure."

Right then my friend Jared joined us. We knew each other since elementary school. He managed to become a multimillionaire while still in his twenties, but maintained a frugal lifestyle. Still, he gave away lots of money to some of his down-and-out relatives.

"Aren't you going to introduce me to your friend?" he asked.

"Gwen, I'd like you to meet my oldest friend, Jared."

Gwen curtsied and Jared bowed. "Très enchanté, mademoiselle!"

"Merci beaucoup."

"Hey, if you guys insist on jabbering away in Spanish, I'm outta here," I said.

"Speaking of getting out of here, "said Gwen, "I've got to go. I've got an early morning."

"Gwen's a doctor," I explained.

"What's your specialty?"

"Jared, I'm a pulmonology resident at Bellevue."

"Well, get a good night's sleep."

She smiled, shook hands with both of us, and headed for the door. Jared stood there watching her leave. Then she stopped, turned around, smiled at him, and left.

I had a terrible feeling deep down in the pit of my stomach. "Are you alright, Brad? Forgive the double entendre, but you look like you could use a doctor."

I looked at him. "You really *like* her?"

"*Like? LIKE?* Brad, I think I'm in love. And just like that, I let her walk out of my life."

I didn't say anything. Her card was tucked away in my pocket. Should I *tell* him? *Shit!*

What should I *do?* Jared was my best and oldest friend. But Gwen! I had never seen such a beautiful woman.

Jared looked awful. "Why did I let her walk out of here? You know, when she was halfway to the door, she turned around and smiled at me?"

"Yes, I saw that."

"I should have asked her for her number." As he spoke I could hear the strains of *The Tennessee Waltz* playing in my head. Soon I was close to crying.

"No! I should have taken her arm and left with her."

"Jared. I have to tell you something. I think *I'm* in love with her too."

"Oh my *God!* What a mess!"

"There's more. Before you joined us, she gave me her number and said she would go out with me."

"*Shit!*" Jared then hit his forehead with the palm of his hand several times. Somehow this made me laugh. Pretty soon he was laughing too. People started looking at us. I thought of trying to explain that what set this off was that we were in love with the same girl. Then maybe those two guys Gwen had been talking to would yell out, "Join the club!"

"Brad, please let me apologize if I screwed things up for you."

"I don't think you did. Even if I had been seeing her for a while, I think the same thing would have happened when the two of you met. *Trust* me on this one: she's a lot more attracted to you than to me. End of story."

"So what happens now?"

"Tomorrow I'll give her a call. I'll ask if it's OK for me to give you her number."

"*Great!*"

"One more thing, Jared." I paused here for effect. "Don't fuck this up!"

"Don't worry!"

"I *mean* it, Jared. We both know how cheap you are."

"*Moi!* It's true that I hate to waste money, but I think 'cheap' would be inaccurate. I just hate being taking advantage of."

"You're so worried about someone taking advantage of you that you don't even give them the chance to *not* take advantage."

"Brad, how many times have we had this conversation? There's no shortage of users out there, and I just don't want to be used."

"Look, Gwen is the woman of your dreams. Remember, *that's* the most important thing. So you're getting this chance for a do-over. You're going to be with the girl who just walked out of your life. But you've gotta do the right thing. Gwen is a goddess. You know how much I wish I were in *your* shoes."

"I know that, Brad. I know exactly what you're going through, and I'm really sorry if I messed up your chances with Gwen."

"I appreciate that, but you probably didn't. If she were that hot on me, she never would have even looked at an asshole like you."

Jared reached over and hugged me. *"Brothers!"* we shouted.

'Brothers with different *mothers!*"

"Brothers with different *fathers!*"

OK Jared, I'm gonna call it a night. I'll call you as soon as I talk to her."

2

The next morning my phone rang at nine o'clock, waking me up. "Hello?"

"Hello, Brad. This is Gwen."

"Gwen, I thought you were at work."

"I am. Brad. I am so embarrassed."

"I know you are. So please, you don't need to be."

"Really?"

"You're calling because you like my friend Jared."

"Oh Brad, I'm *so* sorry!

"Don't be. I appreciate your honesty. And I'm very happy to tell you that Jared feels the same about you."

"*Does* he? Brad, I just couldn't help myself. As soon as he joined us, I felt this tremendous attraction. He's so charismatic!"

"That he *is*!"

"So may I have his number?"

"Of course! As soon as you left the party, he got really depressed. He said that the girl of his dreams had just walked out of his life. So I told him you had given me your number and that I would call you to ask if it would be OK for me to give it to him."

"Brad, I feel so terrible about this. I did not want to hurt you."

"Look, Gwen, you've gotta go with your feelings. I'm very happy for the two of you."

"You may not be a theatrical agent, but you *do* have a flare for the dramatic."

"Well, I don't know about that, but I love happy endings. Promise me that you and Jared will invite me to your wedding."

"*Invite* you? You'll be our best man—*and* our maid of honor."

"Great! But what could I possibly wear?"

3

About half an hour later my phone rang. As soon as I heard her voice, I knew what had happened.

"You'll never guess what just happened!"

"Wanna bet?

"I called Jared. He was really glad to hear from me."

"I knew he would be."

"We talked about how awkward everything was, and how nice and understanding you were. I can see why the two of you have been best friends."

"Yeah, Jared and I *do* go back."

"So we made a date to meet at this Chinese restaurant near my apartment—The Mandarin Palace." Oh *shit!* I knew exactly what was coming, even though I had warned him not to do it!

"And then, just as we were about to hang up, he grew very agitated. I thought he might be having an anxiety attack."

"He really sounded *that* upset?"

"*Upset?* Trust me: this was not the first anxiety attack I've seen—or heard over the phone.

"I told him to try taking deep breaths. I could hear him doing that. In a minute or so, his breathing had become much more normal."

"I know Jared has some allergies, but I never knew he had anxiety attacks. What do you think set it off?"

"That's an excellent question, Brad. Anxiety about almost anything can trigger an attack. When Jared was breathing more normally, I asked if he could tell me what had upset him."

"There was just silence, except for his breathing. I waited. And then, suddenly, he blurted it out: 'We're going *Dutch*, right?'"

4

Over the next year or so, Jared and I worked out an implicit "Don't ask, don't tell" policy regarding Gwen. I knew that he knew that I knew what had happened between them. Enough not said.

I knew that I had never had any claim on her, and that she and Jared had both felt terrible about hurting me. But even after all this time, I was *still* hurting. My only consolation was that I had not tried to stand in their way. Deep down, beneath my crassly superficial exterior, there beats the bleeding heart of a true romantic.

What galled me so much about Jared was not that he had "stolen" Gwen away from me, but that after I'd given him a second chance, he fucked it up exactly the same way he had done so many times before. And I knew then that he would continue to play the same tired old record.

But then, Jared truly surprised me when we got together one evening for dinner. I knew there was something on his mind, and that he would tell me in his own good time.

"Brad, we've known each other for so long, but I'll bet you never knew about my anxiety attacks."

I just looked at him. Was he going to bring up what had happened with Gwen? I braced myself. But when I saw the broad grin on his face, I began to relax.

"I don't have to tell you that I have issues with being afraid of being taken advantage of. But I never connected them with these anxiety attacks."

"How long have you been having them?"

"As long as I can remember."

"What happens?"

"Well, certain times, when one is coming on, I get this shortness of breath, and feel I'm losing control."

"So, are you going to a doctor?"

"Actually, I've been seeing a psychiatrist."

"Really?"

"Brad, you're the only person who knows this. I know you won't tell a soul."

"Of course not!"

"I know that. But I think I was supposed to *say* that."

Just then the waiter came over with the check. In one smooth move, Jared just nodded at him without even looking at the check, and handed him his credit card. Then we looked at each other and burst out laughing.

When I got home, I thought that maybe there was hope for all of us after all. Who would have thought that Jared could ever even *begin* to work out his problems? Maybe it was time for me to begin to get on with my life.

That long-ago party had changed our lives—and his for the better. Well, why not mine? So I decided to go back to that party, at least in my mind.

I had walked into the party, staked out Gwen, got her to come over to me—and *then* what? Why did I have to play games instead of being straight with her? My stupid theatrical agent card, the dumb line about the escaped mental patients? Why didn't I just blurt out how I felt about her? Or was I just too busy being a jerk?

Maybe I needed to change just as much as Jared did. Then I smiled, thinking that at least I gave my best friend a second chance, even though *I* would never get one.

Maybe you're thinking, why not just try calling her? She might even be glad to hear from me, and who knows—even go out with me. But then, there would be what happened between them still hanging over us. I knew I would never make that call.

One day I got an e-mail that really made me laugh:

Dear Brad,

You must get this all the time, so I'm sure you're already thinking that I'm just another poor actress who desperately needs a theatrical agent. So I'm going to make you an offer you can't refuse. Have dinner with me Friday at eight at the restaurant of your choice? My treat.

This must be some kind of practical joke. Or maybe it's Jared trying to trick me into going out on a blind date. Still, I liked this person's *chutzpah*. So I wrote back, "Deal! But only if you let me pay."

By Friday evening, I was actually looking forward to my mystery "date." After all, what *else* did I have going on in my social life?

When I walked into The Mandarin Palace, I spotted her immediately. She stood up as I approached. We practically threw ourselves into each other's arms. We clung together as though we would never let go.

I'm not a religious person, but I thanked God. I knew I had been given a second chance.

ABOUT THE AUTHOR

Steve Slavin has a PhD in economics from New York University, and taught economics for 31 years at New York Institute of Technology, Brooklyn College, and New Jersey's Union County College. He has written 16 math and economics books. These include a widely used college textbook now in its eleventh edition, and the bestselling All the Math You'll Ever Need. His short stories have appeared in dozens of literary magazines.